TWIN LEOPARDS

TRESSIE LOCKWOOD

Copyright © July 2012, Tressie Lockwood
Cover art designed by Mina Carter © July 2012
ISBN 978-1-937394-55-4

This is a work of fiction. All characters and events portrayed in this novel are fictitious or used fictitiously. All rights reserved, including the right to reproduce this book, or portions thereof, in any form.

Amira Press
Charlotte, NC
www.amirapress.com

Whisper

Chapter One

"Whisper, wake up," came the voice through a hazy fog in her brain. Whisper moaned and tried to sink further into sleep. Someone flicked her nose, and she swatted out blindly. "Whisper, damn it, wake the hell up!"

She jerked and opened her eyes. Her best friend, Sheila, sat on the side of her bed still in the slinky red dress she'd worn on her date out. Whisper yawned and rubbed her eyes. "What?" she grumbled. "You know how hard it is for me to fall asleep. Why do you want to mess with me when I finally get there?"

Sheila sucked her teeth and rolled her eyes. "I wanted to tell you about my date."

"And it couldn't wait until the morning?"

"No, now get up." She tugged Whisper's arm until she was in a sitting position on the queen size bed. Then her friend took up the spot next to her and kicked off her shoes. Whisper sighed and offered a bit of her cover.

"Fine, tell me, but if I get fired tomorrow because I'm drooling on the conference room table asleep, you're going to pay my rent."

Sheila sucked her teeth. "Please. You know damn well your boss is into you. He'd give you a raise if you just shook your ass a little for him."

"Which is exactly why I won't!"

Sheila waved her hand. "You have to learn how to use what you got without *using* what you got. If you know what I mean."

Whisper smothered another yawn. "If I knew what you meant, I'd be already using it, and this conversation would be pointless."

"Lawd, girl, why you have to be difficult?"

Whisper squinted at the bedside clock. "Because it's two in the morning."

"So we went to Carrabas, right?" Sheila said as if Whisper hadn't spoken. "And then he said to me—"

Whisper stared at her friend, and Sheila stared back. Something had thumped and crashed in the hall outside her apartment. The noises had been followed by what distinctly sounded like the growl of an animal. Whisper gasped. Pets weren't allowed in her building, and as far as she knew no one had any. All of her neighbors were older, although she remembered Mrs. Stevens had mentioned a new guy moving in across the hall. Whisper hadn't seen or heard him.

"What the hell was that?" Sheila said, casting her voice low.

Whisper tossed her covers aside and rose. "Like I know? Whoever it is better get rid of the animal before the management company finds out. They aren't very tolerant."

As if they'd signaled each other, they both crept on tiptoe toward the front of her small apartment. Whisper reached the peephole first but couldn't see anything. "No one's there."

"I'll get to the bottom of it." Before Whisper could stop her, Sheila wrenched the door open and stepped into the hall. Whisper rushed out after her to jerk her crazy friend back inside, but a man naked from the waist up stopped both of them in their tracks. He stood in the doorway diagonally across from hers and watched them with narrowed dark eyes. Whisper couldn't figure out if they were a deep gray or just downright black. She shivered. Either way, they were sexy as hell but held a hint of danger.

The man said nothing but let his gaze lower. Sheila had paused just ahead of Whisper, so she figured he was checking out her friend's body. Who could blame him when Sheila loved to wear skimpy clothes that accentuated her lithe figure. Boobs the perfect size as well as her round ass and long legs, Sheila always had to beat men off with a stick.

Whisper on the other hand—well, she'd been fighting with the same thirty pounds too many for half her adult life. She loved her friend but, damn, a woman like her couldn't be seen past the diva that was Sheila. Tonight was no exception.

"I suggest you watch your step," Tall-And-Sexy said in a panty-wetting tone.

Whisper glanced down at the floor. Right in front of her place, something glass had shattered. Sheila squealed and leaped to the side. Whisper noticed she'd moved in the direction of Mr. McHottie instead of back into the apartment. *Dang, wasn't she just excited about the date with man number fifty thousand? Now she's set her sights on my new neighbor? Just let me enjoy a little hope that I have a shot for a minute!*

"Oh, let me get a broom and dustpan," Whisper offered. She turned to go back into her apartment, but Sheila wasn't paying her any mind. She walked on tiptoes toward the neighbor, easy for her since she wore stilettos like they were flats. Whisper rolled her eyes and stomped inside.

When she returned, she ignored the two beautiful people chatting with each other and began cleaning up the mess. The more Sheila giggled, the higher her anger rose. The least the idiot could do was thank her. No, he was busy probably looking down Sheila's dress or grabbing her ass or… She grunted in frustration and bent lower to scoop the last bit of glass that had escaped her. A sharp intake of breath made her wonder what happened now.

"Do all the women around here dress this way in public, or just this building?" The cynicism was clear in the man's tone. Whisper peered over her shoulder, and a flutter of panic hit her when she realized the man was aiming his question at her. His gaze was no longer on Sheila but on Whisper's ass. Too late she remembered that she'd been feeling sorry for herself because she had no one in her life and she'd worn the thong panties she'd ordered online from a plus size lingerie site.

She jumped to her feet and yanked her nightie down. The broom and dustpan she let fall, scattering the glass all over the floor again. She took a hasty step toward her door, but he was there in front of her in a heartbeat. She wasn't even sure when he moved or how he could have done it so fast. Maybe she blacked out from embarrassment for a second. His hand was a heavy weight at her back, and then both were about her waist. He raised her like she weighed five pounds, and set her down in her doorway.

Whisper just stood there staring at him while he bent to clean up the mess. Her heart raced, and her head spun from the memory and sensations of having him touch her. He'd smelled so good, delicious enough to eat. If she'd had her head on right, she would have used one of Sheila's numbers and stumbled against him so she could get a feel of that big chest and hard abs. No, she was too busy worrying about him seeing her fleshy butt in a thong. *Mercy! Why me?*

"Um…" she stuttered. If her skin weren't a rich brown, she'd be beet red, she was sure.

"So, baby, you just moved in? What's your name?" Sheila asked, never missing a beat.

The man glanced up at her. Whisper was struck again by his eyes. They were black now that she saw them closer. He didn't appear to be about to answer Sheila's question. His interest was in getting the glass up and getting back to his apartment. When he glanced at Whisper, however, he answered. "My name is Alec Macgregor."

For some reason only when he said his name did she detect the lilt in his speech. Scottish, she guessed. She opened her mouth to say her name, but Sheila zipped to his side once again and held her hand out. "Sheila Tate. This is my friend Whisper Price."

Alec took the proffered hand and shook it. Whisper tried not to notice if he held it a little too long or if he again surveyed her friend's body. She'd seen it happen too often, and most of the time she didn't resent Sheila for being what she was. Whisper wasn't down on herself. She worked hard, was planning to go back to school as soon as her work situation became more stable, and for the most part she took care of herself. She liked her face. Many had commented that it was pretty, which irked her. Hey, she had her pluses, so she wasn't a total freak.

On the other hand, a man like Alec wouldn't give her two thoughts. He stood at least six foot four, was built like a Mac truck, and had thick black hair she wouldn't mind running her fingers through. Just once she had dated a white man, but he turned out to be a dog just like the previous black guys she'd gone out with. Not that there were many. There weren't. Still, she liked to think she was open to whatever package love came wrapped in. Stupid thing hadn't shown up yet, and she was pushing thirty-five.

Alec seemed about ready to turn to her, extricating his hand from Sheila's, when he went stiff looked toward his open apartment door. Whisper followed his line of sight. Damn, he was so eager to get away from them that he was looking longingly toward his new home?

While she peered in that direction, her eyes widened and mouth went dry at the large furry head that popped around the doorway. "What the...?" she murmured. A breeze stirred her hair, and she found Alec zipping back to his apartment.

"You shouldn't be out here," he growled.

She wondered at the way he spoke to the animal as if it would understand every word. Alec reached a hand out, but the animal faked left and darted right to sidestep him. Sheila clamped onto Whisper's arm. Her friend hated pets of all kinds, which was why she was perfectly happy living in her own no pets allowed apartment not far from Whisper's place.

"What the hell is that?" Sheila squeaked, tightening her hold until Whisper winced.

The creature padded on huge paws with slanted eyes that locked on Whisper and her friend. Whisper took a step back, and the animal matched her speed as he advanced. "S-Some kind of cat," she stuttered. "He's not supposed to be here. Pets aren't allowed."

Yeah pet. He looks like a freaking horse!

"Don't run," Alec called out. "You will only incite him. Max, get back in the apartment!"

Whisper frowned. What kind of name was Max for a…a cat? Hell, what kind of cat was so huge? The thing was almost twice the size of a tiger, but it looked like a leopard. The yellow eyes were trained on Sheila, and her friend darted behind her, crying out, "I think it wants to eat me."

As if it understood her words, the beast growled low in its throat and bobbed its head wildly. Just when it got within steps of Whisper, Alec was there, blocking out her view of the cat with his broad back. Whisper couldn't help peering around his arm. The cat roared and leaped, but Alec caught it at the neck. His arm muscles flexed, and if Whisper weren't so scared out of her mind to even move, she could appreciate the man's body.

The two of them—man and animal—stared into each other's eyes as if they held a battle of wills. Whisper couldn't imagine why anyone would keep a pet that was liable to attack like that, even the hand that fed him. Having such an animal as a pet had to be illegal.

"Max, you don't want to do this. I know it hurts, but she's gone, and you have to accept that."

Who is she? Whisper wondered.

"Go back," Alec told the beast again. "Calm down, and we'll talk all night if necessary."

Again Whisper questioned his talking to the cat as if it were human. Too bad the tall sexy man was out of his head. Well, she could enjoy looking at him when he came and went from his apartment. Eye candy couldn't hurt. *Well, unless it comes with a cat big enough to swallow a woman whole.* She shivered.

At last the cat gave a small mewl which sounded like annoyance. From the look of it, it had not intended to hurt Alec at all. The beast had wanted to scare them. Boy had it succeeded. The whole demeanor, the stiff, rippling muscles seemed to relax, and it dropped down to all fours. With another glance in Sheila's direction, the cat turned and padded back to Alec's apartment to disappear through the doorway. Whisper thought she heard a collective sigh from the other two along with her own.

If Whisper thought they were going to get an apology for the near mutilation, she was going to be waiting forever. Rather than say a word, Alex half spun in their direction, gave a curt nod, and disappeared after his pet. Whisper's mouth dropped open, and Sheila swore.

"Who the hell does he think he is?" her friend demanded. "Um-uhn, ain't that much sexy in the world for me to put up with that kind of treatment without a I'm sorry or something!"

She started off as if she intended to bang on Alec's closed door, but Whisper grabbed her arm. "Are you insane, girl? Did you see that thing? If you piss him off, he might just sic it on you."

"I think he should be reported."

Whisper pulled her back to the apartment. "Probably. Tonight though, I'm going back to bed. You sleeping over?"

Sheila crossed her arms over her chest and stomped into Whisper's living room. Sometimes when Sheila was out, she'd have her dates drop her at Whisper's place, and they would chat into the wee hours. Then Sheila would sleep on the pull out couch, and Whisper in her bed until noon. They would get up, shower, and make an elaborate breakfast of waffles, eggs, bacon, and sausage. Now that she thought of it, Whisper figured that's why she could never lose the extra weight. Sheila could eat whatever she wanted. Whisper couldn't.

"Yeah, I'm staying." She walked over to the couch and began tossing pillows on the floor. When she was done, she swung around to wag a finger at Whisper. "But you better believe in the morning, his ass is toast."

Whisper rolled her eyes. "Why do I feel like you're more annoyed that the cat interrupted your play with Alec than anything else?"

"Please. Alec Macgregor and his giant leopard are nothing. Soon enough, they will be gone, and we won't have to deal with them ever again."

Chapter Two

Alec stood in the doorway to his brother's room and frowned at the man sleeping half on, half off the bed. He ran a hand through his hair and sighed. On one hand he realized his brother was having a hard time, but the man was risking exposure of their existence, which he couldn't allow to happen. Of course, he could never imagine how hard it must be to lose his mate. Alec had never taken a mate. He hadn't even been in love before. Not really. Women to him were for pleasure and nothing to involve his heart or bind himself to. He gave as much as he got, so his outlook didn't make him feel guilty. His tastes varied, and he knew what he wanted when he saw it.

That thought brought up the very delectable African American woman he'd seen in the hall the night before. Her sweet figure, curved in all the right places, had given him a hard-on, but Alec never allowed his physical desires to interfere with what he needed to do. What had been important last night was getting Max into the apartment and out of sight.

While he stood there, his brother's blond head popped above the covers, and he peered at Alec through squinted eyes. "I thought I felt your accusing glare," Max quipped.

"I am not accusing you, Max." Alec pushed off the door jamb and strode across to the window. He threw open the blinds, allowing early morning sunlight to stream in. Behind him, his brother groaned, and he suppressed a grin. "You're letting your emotions get the better of you. We can't allow anyone to know what we are."

"I know that." Max rose naked from the bed. Neither of them were ashamed of their bodies, especially since shifting required no clothes.

"No harm done. They thought you had a pet."

"A leopard? Come on, Max, even if they did believe it, it's against the law to keep such an animal. We agreed when we moved to Virginia we would only shift in a wooded area, not here in the hallway of an apartment building where others can see."

Max pulled on jeans, not caring that he hadn't first put on boxers. "You agreed, not me. I didn't say I wanted to come here. I was happy in Maine."

"Happy?" Alec repeated.

His brother flared his nostrils. "I lived at least."

"With supreme effort on my part." Alec approached his brother and laid a hand on his shoulder. "I don't pretend to know what you feel, but I am here for you. I will get you through this even if I have to put my foot in your ass."

His brother chuckled, a rare occurrence lately. "I'm tearing up at all the love. Anyway, what will we do about the ladies? They threatened to report us."

Alec shrugged. "Let them inspect. They will find nothing, and who will believe I was keeping a four hundred pound leopard here?"

Max grinned. "Good then I can—"

"Keep it under wraps," Alec finished for him.

Max grunted. "You were always the one that played by the rules, Alec. When are you going to let loose and go buck wild? It would do you good. Hell, fall in love for once. Let a woman stomp all over your heart, and then drink all night feeling sorry for yourself. It's life."

Alec turned to leave the room. "Yeah, that doesn't sound like fun. I'll pass. I have some work to take care of, so I'll see you later. Stay out of trouble." He waved over his shoulder and left.

* * * *

Alec had been putting off laundry for a while. Usually his shirts went to the cleaners, but there were always the jeans and slacks. He'd taken his laptop down to the laundry room. Maybe he couldn't get good reception for the Internet there, but he could work on the novel he'd been developing for the last couple of years. If Max knew about it, he'd rib him to no end. Not like the book was a romance or anything. His interest was in a thriller, and since he'd had the idea, he decided to see where he could take it. Up until then, no one knew what he was doing in his spare time. Alec had a lot of confidence in what he could do making real estate deals. Writing wasn't the same, but he didn't think he sucked at it either.

The first couple of loads started, he settled in leaning on the washing machine and booted up his laptop. Scenarios ran through his mind of the direction he wanted to take the book. When the click of heels sounded in the hallway, he looked up from the words on the screen. He pressed his lips together at the sight of the woman from a couple nights ago.

"Well, hello, stranger," she said in a husky tone that grated more than turned him on. "Fancy seeing you here."

He turned his gaze back to the computer screen. "I live in the building. It stands to reason I'd have to do laundry sometime."

If he thought his gruff attitude would put her off, he was mistaken. She sauntered over to him, and he observed her figure—slender and sexy. She'd worn shorts that showed off her long legs and a top cut so low, he didn't need a writer's imagination to guess the little that was hidden. He liked a sexy, beautiful woman, but this one wasn't his type. Now her friend—he couldn't get the sight of her bent over wearing a thong out of his head. Her lush figure, slightly plump, and the sweet embarrassment that had been clear in her expression afterward told him Whisper was someone he'd like to pursue.

The woman in front of him moved closer. He searched his mind for her name. *Sheila*. A slow grin spread over her face, revealing even white teeth that must be the product of braces. "I notice you like what you see." She bumped his thigh with her hip. The woman couldn't know whatever expression had been on his face, it was in remembering Whisper not her.

"I admit you're an attractive woman." He let the indifference stand plain in his tone. "However, I'm not interested."

Anger flashed in her eyes before she hid it behind a smile and swatted his arm. "Playing hard to get is for women, not guys. Anyway, tell me how you got out of the super finding your pet. Did you hide him in a closet or something?"

"I'm not sure what pet you're referring to." Annoyance burned in him, but he kept his teeth ground together to avoid saying more.

Sheila eyed him with her lips turned up and chuckled. "Oh okay, it's like that? I hear you. Well, I guess you greased his palm or something. Not like he owns the place anyway. I don't knock people for their fetishes. I have a few of my own."

Shock at what she'd just insinuated made his jaw slack, and he couldn't utter a word. Did any man go for this type of woman? *Ever?* All of a sudden Alec couldn't concentrate on his work if he tried. He turned from the woman and powered down his laptop. After he'd snapped it closed, he started past her. He could come back and check when he thought his clothes had finished their cycle.

"If you'll excuse me…" He moved to squeeze by her, but she pressed closer. Alec would need to toss her roughly aside to get past, and he didn't manhandle women.

Sheila's hands came up around his waist, and she peered at him with wide innocent eyes. Too late she'd already opened her mouth. There was no innocence there. Maybe if he kissed her she would back off. He berated himself for the idiocy of the thought. That would only encourage her.

"I think we could have a lot of fun," she breathed, the husky quality in her voice, as if he'd taken her breath away.

"I—" he began, but an exclamation behind Sheila caught his

attention. He glanced up and cursed in silence. Whisper stood in the doorway, staring in startled stillness at the two of them. He didn't have to imagine what she thought of the scene she'd just stumbled onto.

"I'm sorry. I didn't mean to interrupt," she said, and spun on her heel.

This time, Alec swore out loud. He shoved Sheila from him. Impulse made him take a step to follow Whisper, but Sheila's words stopped him.

"If you're thinking about going after my friend, you should know she has a boyfriend." She waved a hand. "But I don't guess a man like you would go after *her*."

Alec thought better of going after Whisper at that moment. He needed to be sure of whether she had a boyfriend. He didn't desire nor have a need to horn in on another man's territory. His people took that type of thing very seriously, probably the leopard in him. Sheila's attitude toward her friend was no better though.

"Does she know you think so highly of her?"

For the first time, he saw a flash of guilt in her expression. Again it disappeared behind the mask she wore. "It's not like that. Whisper is my home girl. We go way back, and I protect her. She couldn't handle what you're bringing." Sheila leaned on a dryer and folded her arms over her chest. The move only highlighted and raised her breasts. He didn't find it interesting. "I mean you're not looking to have a relationship with her or anything, or am I mistaken?"

That gave him pause. She was right. He wasn't going to pursue a relationship with Whisper. He just wanted a little fun, something he was sure to return. He didn't think of himself as arrogant—not wholly anyway—but he did believe he could give her some of the greatest pleasure she'd ever experienced. That reasoning came from his feeling that sex wasn't good unless both parties were pleased.

"What I intend to do with Whisper isn't your business," he quipped.

"Oh so it's Whisper." The resentment rolled off the woman. "You remember her name from the other night. Guess a flash of a thong would get any man hot and bothered." She raised a defiant chin to him. If this woman didn't have such a bad attitude, she could be a perfect beauty. As it was, with each word from her lips, she turned him off. He was not the type of man who was into bitches, and a bitter woman had no appeal to him. The limited interaction he'd had with Sheila told him all he needed to know about her. "How about you play with me?" she offered.

Alec resisted rolling his eyes. "No." He leaned closer to her upturned face and narrowed his gaze. "Are you so desperate?"

Her mouth dropped open, and she raised a hand to smack him, but he caught it and shoved it away. "Asshole!"

He gave a slight bow as if to acknowledge the insult but allow it to roll off his back. Now he wanted to get at Whisper all the more. He knew Sheila was the wrong reason, but so be it. "If you'll excuse me."

Alec pushed past Sheila with the intention of never thinking of her again.

Chapter Three

Whisper was determined more than ever to lose weight. After she'd walked in on Alec and Sheila in the laundry room looking like they were about to kiss, she figured she had to do something about her weight. Hell, about her whole wardrobe and outlook. She'd been comfortable in frumpy tops and baggy pants for too long. If she didn't like the way she looked, then, damn it, she needed to get the extra weight off. That started with taking up jogging again. She'd done it for a while last year and dropped fifteen pounds, but then her knee started bothering her, and instead of taking it easy until it was better, she'd dumped exercise altogether. That wasn't happening this time.

She had intended to go while it was still daylight after work, but her boss had kept her later than usual. She was getting tired of all the overtime since overtime pay had been frozen for the foreseeable future. The man spouted nonsense about doing what was good for the company and them all being one big family, but she didn't see his ass suffering any losses.

By the time she got off work, the sun was fast going down, but there were plenty of people in the park doing the same thing she was, so she wasn't worried about it. As long as she stayed on the lighted paths, things would be fine, and she wouldn't be out there long.

On a bench, she re-tied her sneakers, adjusted her shorts, which now that she thought about it might not have been the best choice, and then started a slow walk that became a slow jog. Soon she was lost in her head, enjoying the evening breeze of late spring. Tonight she hadn't wanted to wear her headphones. Music blaring in her ears would take away from her peace rather than add to it. On another day, she might feel differently.

TWIN LEOPARDS – Tressie Lockwood

At a split in the trail, she took the right without thinking. Only when she'd jogged a good twenty minutes did she remember this one took her deeper into the wooded area. She was still in the city, but fewer joggers took this way at night. The lighting was strong, but she didn't want to take a chance. *I am not getting my fifteen minutes of TV fame because I'm in a body bag.*

She stopped jogging and took her pulse, then turned around. A man standing in the path brought a small scream to her lips. He was stark naked. Whisper stumbled backward with a hand up to her mouth. Her heart hammered in her throat, and she thought she would pee her panties. While she backed up and the man watched her with curious narrowed eyes saying nothing, another man moved from the trees. He was clothed, and his focus was on the naked man.

"Damn it, Max, put your clothes on. I told you it was a little too early to come out here." The second man tossed the first a duffle bag. A few moments passed before Whisper recognized him. Alec.

"What the—" she muttered. Alec swiveled his head to face her, and his eyebrows went up. Whisper didn't even wait for an explanation. She pivoted on her heel and jetted. These guys were crazy, or gay, or both. She had to tell Sheila. Not that her girlfriend was in danger of losing her heart over Alec, but damn, what were they doing? And would they kill her for finding out their secret? *Whatever secret it is.*

Fear pushed her to run faster, and rather than stay on the path where the light would give away her location, she leaped over a railing and crashed through the brush. Man, she should get an Olympic gold medal for that jump. She almost laughed at the absurdity of her thoughts and realized she was hysterical. Blood pulsed loud in her ears so she couldn't hear if anyone pursued her. She figured out real quick that they were when strong hands grabbed her arms and hauled her off her feet. Whisper screamed.

"Shh, it's okay, Whisper," Alec muttered in her ear. "I promise I'm not going to hurt you, but it's dangerous for you out here alone."

"Yeah, because of crazies like you! Get off of me." She kicked at his legs, but he didn't even wince as she struggled to get free.

While she fought, the other man came through the trees just pulling his shirt over a muscled chest. Whisper bit her tongue to keep from crying out in terror. They were going to kill her together and dump her body somewhere.

"I won't tell anyone," she assured them. "I didn't see anything."

"You're right you didn't," snapped the other man.

Alec's hand spread over her belly as if he protected her. "Back off, Max. I'll handle this.

The other man looked a lot like Alec except with blond hair. "Do you really think you can get her into your bed after scaring the shit out of her?"

"Bed," Whisper shrieked. She fought harder to get away. Somehow she got her teeth into the space between his thumb and forefinger and bit down. Alec grunted, and his hold loosened. Whisper broke free and ran forward. The other man zipped from where he was and stood in front of her. He brought a heavy hand down on her shoulder and did something with his fingers. Whatever it was, it hurt, and Whisper whimpered before everything went dark, and she crumpled to the ground.

* * * *

Whisper shifted and moaned. She came alert slowly, registering the sounds around her. With Alec and the man he'd called Max speaking above her, she came to realize that she was in Alec's arms being carried. All she could think about was how heavy she must be and her big butt in those stupid shorts hanging in midair for all the world to see.

She opened her eyes and glanced up at him. His mouth was set in a determined line, and his brows hung low over his eyes. The anger that radiated off of him couldn't be missed, but he seemed not to have broken a sweat or to be straining carrying her. She started to ask him to put her down when she peered across to Max who walked next to him. The man who had done something to her shoulder was sporting a black eye.

"I can't believe you sided with her over your own brother," the man complained.

His brother? No wonder they looked alike. So maybe they weren't gay. They were still crazy, and now that she'd calmed down enough to think rather than react, maybe she could get herself out of this mess.

"It's not a matter of siding," Alec answered. "You hurt her, a defenseless woman. You used to show a lot more finesse than that, but I'm not going to cover for you any longer. Time to wake up and take responsibility for your actions."

The other man sneered. "Excuse me for grieving the loss of the only woman I'll ever love."

"Grieve all you want. Hurt Whisper again, and I will rip your arm off and feed it to you."

His brother gave a dramatic shiver. "You almost have me believing you care about her. But that would be impossible for the consummate bachelor, Alec Macgregor. Unless of course she was your…mate."

"Shut up!" Alec groused.

Whisper mulled over all they'd said. On the one hand, she couldn't help the warm and fuzzies at the way Alec protected her. He'd actually hit his brother, whom he must have known all his life, for her who he'd just met. She mentally shook her head. No, he was crazy, and she couldn't forget the part about Alec being a consummate bachelor or that Max had said all Alec wanted was to get her in bed. Why her when he could have Sheila in a heartbeat? Thinking of her friend, she remembered the two of them in the laundry room. That tossed cold water on her thoughts, and she looked up at Alec with a frown.

"You can put me down now," she demanded more than asked.

Alec stopped walking and hesitated. He seemed to be puzzling over

Whisper

something as he stared at her. Whisper fidgeted, and he at last gave in. Once on her feet, she missed the warmth of his arms. The night had grown slightly chilly, and the two big men were cast in shadows no matter how much the path they were on was lighted. Only the stars illuminated the sky because the moon was hidden behind thick clouds.

"I want you to know I'm pressing charges for assault," she announced and then regretted it. How many times had she yelled at a heroine in a novel not to say stupid stuff when she was in the middle of nowhere with the enemy? She couldn't count the number of times.

Alec stood stiff and unreadable. "You'd be in your right to do so, but can I ask that you forgive my brother? I will make up for what he did in any way necessary."

Whisper swung her gaze from one man to the other. Max didn't appear in a hurry to apologize. In fact, he seemed quite content for Alec to take the weight of it. She hated people with relationships like that. She couldn't respect them. The person being used was just as bad as the user.

She couldn't help putting her hands on her hips and sassing the man. Her common sense must have gotten knocked out of her head when she hit the ground. "Make it up how, by offering yourself to me?" Embarrassment almost knocked her out again at the amusement on both their faces. She *so* couldn't play the games that Sheila played with men. "I mean…"

"If that's what you want," Alec told her without hesitation, "I'm all yours."

She had to save face some way. "Yeah, no thanks. You're not my type. I don't know what kind of freaky game you and your brother play in the park at night, but I want no part. Let's pretend tonight never happened, but stay away from my friend. Good evening, gentlemen."

She spun on her heel and marched away with her head held high. All the time, she expected to hear laughter behind her or some cruel remark about her weight and figure. She heard nothing and sighed with relief when she made it back to her car without any more incidents.

* * * *

Whisper woke in the middle of the night. She held still in bed wondering what had awakened her, but no sound reached her ears. The bedside table sat visible in the pale moonlight, and she noticed that she'd forgotten to bring in her nightly bottle of water. Her room was always too dry, so her throat hurt. Water alleviated the issue, so she kept it near. After tossing back the covers, she rose and yawned, heading toward the kitchen. That's when she heard it. A mewl like an animal in pain.

Without thinking, she rushed to the door, turned the locks, and wrenched it open. There in the hall was the same big cat she'd seen that first night. The beast lay in front of Alec's closed door with its head down and whining like the world had come to an end. Whisper couldn't have said why afterward, but she stepped into the hall and made a clicking sound with her tongue at the roof of her mouth. She held out her hand to the cat.

"Come here, sweetie. It's okay," she called. "Come on, baby."

The leopard lifted its head and peered in her direction. Tiredness must have made her wonky because she could have sworn the cat raised a skeptical eyebrow at her. He looked toward Alec's door and back at her, and then hefted its hugely muscled body to stand. Whisper's heart beat hard in her chest as it neared, but she didn't back off. The cat drew close and nuzzled her hand. A rough tongue lapped her palm, tickling a little.

Whisper turned and headed back into her apartment. The cat watched where it stood. "Coming?" she asked him, and he padded inside. She shut the door promising herself to give Alec a piece of her mind for locking his pet outside like that. He had to have heard him crying.

She led the leopard to her bedroom and pulled a blanket off the bed to toss onto the floor. "You can sleep here. Don't poop or pee in my place, or you and me are going to have a problem."

Again the cat gave her a look like he wouldn't sink so low. Whisper laughed. Tonight, once again, she'd worn the thong panties and a long tee. The shirt rose as she climbed into bed, but she didn't bother pulling it down. The cat didn't know anything. As soon as she'd tossed the covers back and settled in, the leopard leaped in one fluid motion to her bed and laid a big head in her lap.

"What the hell? No, you get on the floor," she commanded. He ignored her.

She rolled her eyes and lay back. If he didn't want to move, there was no way she'd budge him. That was another thing she would skin Alec for, her loss of sleep.

Day came too soon with someone banging at her door. Whisper sprang up, got tangled in the covers, and fell face first over the side of the bed. The leopard mewled behind her and ran his scratchy tongue over her exposed butt cheek. She slapped his muzzle and freed herself.

The banging started up again, and this time Alec called out through the door. Whisper swore. "Is he serious? Got the nerve to have an attitude?"

She stood up. This time, she drew on a robe before going to the door. "You come on. You're probably in big trouble," she said to the cat. He followed, not looking sorry in the least.

"Where is he?" Alec demanded, brushing past her. Whisper suppressed the shiver that raced over her spine from the man's arm touching her nipple. She crossed her arms and followed him.

"Don't mind me. I just live here," she snapped.

Alec ignored her. "Max! What the hell were you thinking?"

Whisper's eyes widened. "Max? You named your cat after your brother?"

Alec seemed confused for a second, and then his expression cleared.

He focused on the cat. "Get back to the apartment now!"

Whisper thought his pet wouldn't go, but then it padded past, moving with grace and controlled power. When it reached her, the cat allowed its thick body to brush her leg. The fur was so soft and comfortable, she didn't move. All the fear she'd felt that first day was gone for some reason. Whisper bent down and let her fingers run over the fur as he passed by.

After the cat disappeared around the doorjamb, she looked up to find Alec glaring at her. The way he clenched his hands at his sides, she thought the man barely kept himself from violence, and she took a step in retreat. Something was messed up about this situation. She should be more afraid of the wild animal.

Alec advanced and stood towering over her. "Don't encourage him. He's not allowed to sleep here." He paused and looked around. "Just where did he sleep?"

Whisper put her hands on her hips. "As if that's any of your business." She frowned. "Goodness, it's not like we're talking about another man and like you're my boyfriend. Max slept in my bed. You have a problem with it, maybe you shouldn't lock your pet out and ignore him when he cries to get in."

If anything, her words seemed to outrage the man more. He stepped closer and grabbed her arms, hauling her to his chest. Whisper couldn't have predicted the kiss, with him being so pissed off, but when his mouth descended on hers, she didn't complain about it either. Alec punished her with his roughness, in the way he devoured her lips and forced her head back.

She tried catching her breath, but he made it impossible when his tongue swept across her bottom lip and then plunged between them. She would have gone on to surrender all to the man if he didn't come to his senses first and release her. Whisper stood there dazed, teetering on her feet and running the back of her hand across her numb lips.

"You had no right…" she began, but who was she kidding? She was

Whisper

all in just as he was a minute ago. She shook her head to clear it and stood straighter. "Why did you do that? No, don't answer. It's bad enough that you have a leopard as a pet, but at least treat him right! I don't know how you got out of the super finding him because it's not like his big butt can fit in any of these apartments' closets, but I will find someone to take him away if you do that again. You better be glad the other tenants on this floor are elderly and can't hear a hurricane let alone a mewling cat in the hall."

To her surprise, Alec chuckled. "Let me take you to dinner."

"Wha—"

"Dinner," he repeated and moved closer. Whisper backed up. She hit the wall, unable to go any farther unless she wanted to look like an idiot scooting along the narrow entry leading to her living room.

"I-I don't think that's a good idea," she began.

"What's a good idea?" Sheila stood in the doorway. "Wait, Whisper, shouldn't you be at work by now? I came by to get my pink blouse I left over here last time. Thought you'd be gone. It's almost nine."

"Oh crap." Whisper spun on her heel, leaving Alec standing there and ran toward her room. She was already late, and if her boss was in an ugly mood, she was in for it. That's all she needed.

Inside her room, she stripped off the robe and followed it with her T-shirt and thong. With the shower going, she went through her morning regime for her face. Sheila came in and stood in the doorway watching. Whisper fidgeted. She loved her friend, but she was glad she'd slipped a towel on.

"So what was he doing here?" Sheila asked. Whisper picked up on the irritation beneath the casual question.

"Looking for his cat," Whisper told her.

Sheila rolled her eyes. "Well stay away from him, girl. He's bad news. Trust me on this. I know men, and it comes off him in droves."

"Really?" Whisper eyed her friend in the reflection from the mirror. "Because it looked like in the laundry room y'all were about to get to it."

Sheila sucked her teeth. "Please. When I go after a man, he's gotten. I've never been turned down because I do the dropping before we even gets to that point."

Whisper had no idea why Sheila would be talking about being turned down and dropping. They weren't talking about that, but she let it go. Sometimes there was no understanding her friend's mind, so she didn't even try. "Well don't worry about it. I'm not trying to go out with Alec Macgregor or his crazy ass brother."

Sheila frowned. "Brother?"

With a grin, Whisper dropped her towel and hopped into the shower. Although it was a hollow victory that didn't mean a thing, she felt pretty good at getting the last word in a discussion with Sheila. The feeling wouldn't last long, but it was nice for now. Besides, she hadn't lied. She and Alec weren't a good mix even if he was an excellent kisser.

Chapter Four

Whisper pinched the bridge of her nose and rubbed her eyes. They burned something fierce, and all she wanted to do was go home and soak in a hot tub before falling into bed. Of course she had to work late. She suspected the whole "urgency" of the project she was working on was because she'd come in late, and her boss wanted to punish her for it. Still, she couldn't complain. The man hadn't fired her. With so many people out of work and looking, this was not the time to be messing up.

"Whisper, how's it going?"

She jumped when her boss's hands came down on her shoulders. Damn, she hated touchy-feely people who couldn't keep their hands to themselves. Especially bosses who got a little too happy with it.

Trying to be subtle, she wiggled away from his touch and leaned forward to grab a sheet from her desk. "It's fine. I just finished this last spreadsheet. We can go over it tomorrow morning if you want."

He came around from behind her and perched on the edge of the desk. "Why don't we discuss it over dinner?"

Whisper tried not to focus on the glare coming off of his bald head. She thought some men without hair were sexy, but Mr. Peters' head was shaped funny, not hot in the least. The man didn't believe in wiping down the sweat either, which seemed to collect up there.

"Oh, I can't." She thought up a lie. "My boyfriend has been holding dinner for me. I can't disappoint him again after working so late every night the last few weeks." There, she'd thrown in that she'd gone way beyond the call of duty.

He reached for her hand with an insincere smile if ever she saw one.

"Cancel one more time. This is important."

"No."

The muscles in her stomach tightened. *This is not the time to make a stand, Whisper. Just say yes and get it over with.* The thought of spending even half an hour in a casual setting with this man was more than she could deal with. In fact, she slipped her hand from his as quickly as she could. Rumor had it that Mr. Peters' last assistance went to Human Resources about his inappropriate behavior and had gotten fired for it. She suspected there was a lot more to the story, namely the assistant being unable to prove a thing. She wasn't going down that same road, and so far she'd been able to avoid situations like this. Sometimes she felt like Mr. Peters bided his time for when she messed up to take advantage of it, or to collect data to use against her.

At her words, his bushy eyebrows rose. "No?" He apparently couldn't believe she would turn him down.

She heaved a deep breath and searched for an excuse, but somehow nothing came to mind. Enough was enough, and she just couldn't make herself smile and put him off again. His attitude added to her stress, and it wasn't fair. Even if she didn't have proof and it was his word against hers, she couldn't take it anymore.

Thinking that way brought tears to her eyes. Tears of frustration more than anything. She lowered her gaze to her desktop and stared at her hands. Sometimes when she was really angry, her fingers shook, and she cried a little. She hated it because it came off as a sign of weakness, which she resented. "I—"

"Whisper." The rumbling tone sent chills of delight down her spine and brought with it the memory of the kiss they'd shared that morning. "You've kept me waiting long enough, don't you think?"

Her mouth dropped open, and she turned her head to peer in the direction of Alec's voice. He stood near the bank of elevators, which wasn't far from her cubicle. She couldn't remember hearing the ding of the elevator arriving. Most people had gone for the day about half an hour before, so she couldn't imagine how Alec had gotten in or who had told him which floor she was on. The small company's directory hadn't been updated yet, and her unit had moved from floor two to floor five.

"Alec," she murmured. Why did the use of his name have to sound so breathy and sexually excited? "What—"

He pushed off the wall he'd been leaning against and started toward her. She could only watch his progress, along with her boss, in silence. Something about Alec's presence kept them in wait for his next command, as if they were under his spell. Alec moved with the same quiet grace as his leopard. Maybe they'd practiced together. The thought would have been funny if she wasn't mesmerized by the strain of muscle in his thighs, discernible with each step he took. She tried not to notice the thickness of his package at the front his slacks. He might not be erect, but he was definitely working with more than the average man.

When he reached her, Alec extended a hand similar to what her boss had done. This time, Whisper was compelled to put her hand in his. He pulled her to her feet, and she found herself pressed to his chest. He lowered his head in one smooth motion to claim her lips. For a second, she thought he would kiss her as deeply as he had done that morning. That would be embarrassing and inappropriate for where they were. Alec brushed her lips with his in a swift but sensual kiss. Just as before, it swept her breath away.

His hot gaze met hers when he lifted his head. "Let's go." Alec flicked his gaze from Whisper to her boss, and the open desire from a second before turned hard. "I'm sure you don't have a problem with that?"

How could so much threat be stuffed into one question? She didn't know, but it was plain in Alec's bearing and his words. Mr. Peters shifted his shoulders to cover a quiver. The fact that anyone could take the man's power in a heartbeat blew her away. She had to thank Alec for that if nothing else.

"No-no, of course not," Mr. Peters stuttered. "We're done for the night. I was just telling Whisper to go on and get out of here. Can't keep her boyfriend waiting."

Alec made an affirmative noise before focusing on Whisper. At his questioning expression, she hopped to gathering her things. She couldn't believe she was getting out of there at a reasonable hour, and she hadn't had to go to dinner with Mr. Peters.

Within a few minutes, they were in the elevator heading down to the first floor. She turned to Alec. "I never agreed to have dinner with you."

"I took it as an understood," he replied but didn't take his eyes off the floor numbers lighting up as they passed.

"Arrogant of you," she quipped.

He didn't deny it.

Out on the sidewalk, Alec gestured to his car, a sporty number. Whisper hesitated but then got in when he opened the passenger door. Hell, she didn't have to go to dinner with him, but it was late, and she didn't feel like driving. *Sure, girl, tell yourself that. You know damn well you want to kiss him some more.*

They moved out into the traffic. "Anywhere in particular you'd like to go?" he asked.

"Not really."

He chose Ruby Tuesday, and she didn't have a problem with it. Once they were seated in a booth, Whisper hid behind her menu trying to calm her racing pulse. She'd been on plenty of dates, and some of the men were fine. For some reason, Alec both scared and excited her at the same time. She didn't know if she wanted to run away from him or pull him closer. Either way, her body desired more of his touch and the kiss that stole all resistance with a single caress.

"So why the leopard?" she asked after they'd placed their order and Whisper was sipping a cosmopolitan while Alec was having sweet tea. She felt bad for him, but admired his dedication to not drinking and driving.

At her question, he flicked his gaze over her as if speculating on how to answer. "Why aren't you afraid of him?"

Whisper rolled her eyes. "Please, I'm scared of him all right. He's monstrous huge, and when I first saw him, I thought he was going to eat me. I don't know. There's something in his eyes. I guess that look might be why you talk to him like he's human. He understands everything you say, doesn't he?"

While she spoke her tone heightened, and she got excited by what she was saying. She found it to be true, that she liked the big cat, and her fear had lessened. Somehow he had communicated to her that he wouldn't hurt her, which was absurd, but she believed it. Whisper looked at Alec for confirmation, and he nodded.

"He won't hurt you. Max knows I would gut him." He focused on her after draining his glass and setting it down. "I don't want to talk about my brother…uh…or the cat. Tell me more about you."

Whisper smirked. He wasn't getting off that easy. She fully intended to ask him about the naked park running, which was what she concluded they were doing the other night. She still thought it was creepy and weird, but she couldn't deny she was still attracted to Alec.

"Nothing really to tell. I don't have much family. My parents passed years ago, and they were each only children. I have a sister I'm not close to. I hardly ever see Trinity. Sometimes we break down and see each other at Christmas, but that's quick. It looks like you and your brother are close, and I admire that."

Alec acknowledged her words with a gesture but seemed to refuse the bait of talking about Max, so she went on.

"As you saw, I work for a small international trading company. I'm an assistant." She frowned. "How did you get into the building anyway?"

"I have my secrets."

She pursed her lips. "Picking locks included?"

He chuckled, but she noticed he didn't deny it. "I'm good at influencing people when I want to."

"Yeah, uh huh." She rolled her eyes. "Anyway, that's all I can think to say about myself. Pretty boring, I guess."

He took her by surprise when he reached a hand out to stroke her cheek. Whisper froze. She liked the sensations he created a little too much. No, he couldn't possibly want her, especially after he'd been about to get Sheila. How could she forget that little fact?

"You're far from ordinary," he commented when she drew away.

Whisper lowered her eyes to her plate. "You keep coming on to me, but I don't mess with my friend's men, and she doesn't mess with mine." The statement wasn't wholly true, but she didn't care to revisit the past.

"I assure you, I'm not your friend's man." The bite in his tone startled her. She stared at him, and he softened his tone. "What you thought you saw in the laundry room wasn't what it looked like."

She opened her mouth to say something, but he cut her off.

"I'm interested in you, Whisper, *not* your friend."

In which of my fantasies?

"I'm flattered, but I'm not really looking to get into a relationship right now. I have to get work straight, and I'm planning to go back to school the minute my schedule is predictable."

"I wasn't offering a relationship."

Of course not.

"I'm not looking for casual sex either." She leaned back and gathered her purse, about to rise. He stopped her with one of his big hands covering hers. To her embarrassment, it trembled under his. She wasn't sure if it was anger, disappointment, or excitement. Maybe it was a mix of the three. They never wanted more than a roll in the sack. Where did the women who were married to amazing guys for years find them? Whisper's selection of men was way less than Sheila's, but she couldn't count on one hand the ones who had wanted a real relationship. That was because there hadn't been any. She sometimes feared if she found something long term, she wouldn't know how to handle it.

"You drive a hard bargain," he complained with a half smile that did funny things to her insides.

"This isn't a negotiation."

He released her hand and sat back when she didn't bolt. The way he studied her with those dark eyes made her want to fidget. She didn't want him to know how he affected her, so she held perfectly still. Only after her itching nose tormented her did she think about how false that looked, too.

"Five dates," he announced at last.

"Excuse me?"

He grinned. The man must have used that smile to fell many stronger women than she. "Promise me five dates, and if after the fifth you don't want to sleep with me, then I will walk away. I won't pressure you at all."

Whisper pursed her lips. "Are you for real? You're going to sit there and put a number of dates on when I have to sleep with you? Every smart woman knows she doesn't sleep with a guy until she's sure he doesn't just want her for her body and nothing else."

"And I've just dispelled the question for you by saying it *is* what I want," he countered. "However, like I said you don't *have* to sleep with me. You can walk away. I want casual. You don't. At the most, you can enjoy my company, get a few free dinners out and maybe have some fun. All without obligation."

Whisper frowned and shook her head. "Something about this is jacked up. I can't put my finger on it. I guess I have to give you props for getting the whole thing out there in the open, but I should be running for the hills."

He gestured toward the exit. "You are free to leave at any time."

She made as if to go to see if he'd stop her again. He remained seated, relaxed, and too damn sexy for *her* own good. She should be pissed off at him saying some mess like after five dates, he wanted her to put out, but somehow the reaction wasn't the same with him being honest and straightforward about it. Maybe this was the way he lured women in, with twisted proposals they couldn't wrap their heads around. Then again, glancing at his full head of silky dark curls, the strong line of his jaw and full lips, the awesome build, he didn't need a line to get a lot of women to spread their legs. Whisper was tempted to say, "Fuck it, my place or yours." However, there was the question of her body. Alec was perfection itself. She was a whole other matter. With little money, dreams of a tummy tuck was just that—a dream. Her boobs were saggy, and she couldn't even blame it on having kids. She was just plain chunky and scared to show him her body. He could run out of the room in horror.

So I should just say no and leave right now.

"Okay, five dates," she agreed. What was she thinking? "You can't be skimpy in taking me out and letting me have fun. We get to do whatever I want, and you don't push for more, or get happy with your hands."

"Deal." There was that smile again. Goodness, if she wasn't careful, she'd give it up tonight.

"Okay, tell me about you," she encouraged him to distract herself.

His knowing look said volumes. The man was too confident. She'd love to knock him on his ass and make him fall madly in love with her. *Ha ha. Real fantasy, Whisper.*

She listened as she continued eating her food. Alec wasn't just some pretty boy more into his next lay than anything else. She found herself enjoying his stories and him, and that was dangerous.

"Max and I are twins," he said. "I'm older by two hours."

Whisper gaped. "Two hours? I thought you were about to say two minutes."

He chuckled. "I'm sure my mother would have loved it that way, but Max is stubborn. He likes to give everyone around him a hard time and do things his way. I guess he was starting early with all the trouble he gave my mother. I have a younger sister who is married with children. She lives with her family in Maine. That's where Max and I moved down from after…"

She saw pain in his expression, but he masked it and went on. Whisper wasn't sure whether to acknowledge it or let it go, trusting that if he wanted to share he would. In the end, she let him decide.

"He lost his girlfriend recently, a woman who for all intents and purposes was to be his wife. To have her in his life was a big deal for Max. To lose her was more than he could bear for a while."

Whisper made a sympathetic sound. "Sounds like it was hard for you, too."

He gave her a startled glance. "Yes, we all loved her. Sarah became like one of the family. Anyway, I was used to looking out for Max, used to smoothing over whatever feathers he'd ruffled. Things got touchy where we were, so I decided we both needed a change of scenery. We moved here to Virginia."

"Wow, big change. Maine must be really cold in winter and mild during summer? Here it can get hot in summer."

He winked. "I think we can handle it."

For some reason, she blushed. "What do you do for a living?" She didn't figure it paid that much since he lived in her same apartment building.

"We both work in real estate. I wanted to get into the area to be sure of various locations and the best possible place if we decide to buy a house here."

"That makes sense." She hesitated. "Are you planning on always being together? And what do you do naked in the woods?" She slapped a hand over her mouth, eyes going wide. The question just slipped out because she didn't even realize she'd been thinking about it right then.

Alec laughed. He didn't appear to be offended. "No, we're not always going to be together." He raised her hand to his lips and planted

TWIN LEOPARDS — Tressie Lockwood

a light kiss on her knuckles. She shivered. "Trust me, when I have you, I won't want my brother anywhere around."

"*When?*" She sucked her teeth. "You're pretty confident, but don't get excited. I'm firm about where I am in my life." *Lies, all lies. Girl, who are you fooling?*

"I'm hopeful," he said and released her.

Alec went on to discuss all the hair-brained schemes his brother had gotten him into, including the purchase of a money pit of a house—their first—and forged Alec's signature on the paperwork.

"Are you serious? Didn't you want to kill him? Or did you try?"

Alec's gaze clouded a bit as if he recalled just what he'd done. "We have our ways of getting even."

"Hm, I don't like that way that sounds. Remind me not to get on your bad side."

"I wouldn't hurt a beautiful woman like you, Whisper." His tone dropped so deep and rumbly, she shifted in her chair and tried not to think of the state of her panties.

When he went on not answering about the naked woods running, she mentally set a key and lock to her heart. No sir. Sexy was crazy, and she wasn't going down that route. She'd made stupid mistakes in the past with glaring road signs that showed she was headed in the wrong direction. Not again. The dates would be fun for a change because she'd had a long dry spell and was lonely for male companionship. After that, it was over, and Alec could be the stuff of her dreams when she was alone taking care of things with her hand.

She tilted her head to the side and studied him. "Okay, tell me more. Entertain me."

And he did.

Chapter Five

Whisper woke up with her eyes burning. She hadn't slept much the night before because her mind was filled with thoughts of Alec. After dinner, he'd taken her to see a movie. She couldn't have said what the thing was about because she was busy stealing glances at him. Every time she did, she found him looking back. Eventually, he took her hand, and they laced their fingers together. He whispered in her ear, low enough for no one else to be disturbed. She felt like a schoolgirl with a crush, but no matter how hard she fought it, the man charmed her.

"This is why he's so confident," she complained on the way to the bathroom. In the mirror, she frowned at herself. "How many women were right here arguing with themselves to get a grip before it's too late?" Maybe she should cancel the date three days from now. Yeah, she'd been surprised last night at his insistence that they make the next of the five dates as soon as possible. Whisper had had to put up some resistance and suggested three days. Now that she thought of it, maybe three was too eager on her part. *Damn it, I should have said a week.*

An hour later, when she arrived at work, her stomach knotted. She hadn't spoken to Mr. Peters since the night before when he'd been pushed into a corner to allow her to leave with Alec. For all she knew, he'd be pissed and make her life more miserable. She drew in a deep breath as she approached his office and made to pass by with a mere wave and a smile.

"Whisper, come in here a minute," he called.

She stopped cold, and the pain in her belly increased.

"Shut the door," he instructed.

Whisper did as she was asked and took a seat. If she didn't get support under her now, she'd collapse. As she waited for Mr. Peters to finish signing a few papers, she did a running tally of her bills in her mind and tried to determine how long her savings would cover them until she found another job.

Mr. Peters looked up from his papers. "I've decided to restructure your schedule."

She blinked. "Come again?"

"Your schedule." He stood up and moved from behind his desk. Whisper assumed he was going to do his usual, like sit on the edge of his desk way too close to her, or drop a hand on her shoulder and squeeze. Instead, he stood at the window with his back to her and peered out. "I've been unfair to you, Whisper. Just because you don't have a family doesn't mean your time isn't precious to you like the rest of us."

She didn't bother correcting him on the family part. What he said blew her away.

"You'll work until five and not a minute over, Monday through Friday. I insist on it." He smiled as if he'd just done a good deed and was proud of himself. In a way, she guessed he had. "There'll be no need for Mr. Macgregor to miss you unless that's by your choice."

While her boss kept talking, enjoying listening to himself speak, Whisper went over what happened at the office the night before. Alec showed up, and she said his name. Did she say his last name? Of course not. That would be stupid and unnecessary. Who said their supposed boyfriend's last name when they saw him? So how did Mr. Peters know his last name?

"Um, I don't want to interrupt you, Mr. Peters, and I definitely appreciate you cutting out all the overtime for me. Trust me, I can use the extra time for…um…some important things." She decided not to tell him about school. "But how did you know Alec's last name? Did you talk to him?"

Her answer came in Mr. Peters' face going red and a look of fear and horror coming into his eyes. "I-I-I," he stuttered.

She watched him open and close his mouth like a fish and fidget with his shirt collar. Whisper recalled Alec saying he had a way of influencing people when he wanted to. She couldn't help wondering if he'd contacted her boss and threatened him. No, that couldn't be it. He wouldn't know how Mr. Peters would react. Besides, it was just a few dates they had agreed to, nothing serious enough to contact her boss over.

"He or you must have said it last night when he picked you up," her boss lied. She always knew when he wasn't telling the truth. "Anyway, I have a lot of work to get through today, so if you'll excuse me, I'll let you get to yours." He dropped into his chair and mopped his brow with a tattered tissue. "Shut the door on your way out, will you? Thanks."

She had no choice but to leave. She couldn't beat him over the head and demand he tell her what really happened. All day, she pondered it, but no scenario gave her peace. In the end, she decided she was jumping to conclusions and forced herself to let it go.

That evening, Whisper stopped by the school she'd wanted to attend and picked up some information. Her heart beat a rapid tattoo, and she couldn't keep the smile off her face as she entered her building. After going through everything, she would probably find out how to register for classes online. This reprieve in her schedule couldn't come at a better time. She only had a short wait for the next semester to start, and she'd be on her way to a better life.

Stepping out of the elevator on her floor, Whisper hummed as she walked and thought of all the new career opportunities that would someday be hers. She rounded the corner to where her apartment was and bumped into the broad back of the man just coming out of his place. She winced at the pain to her nose.

Max turned around and looked down at her with concern in his eyes. For some reason he appeared a tad less manic today, although she was still struck by how much he looked like Alec. "I'm sorry. Are you okay?"

"Fine, thanks." She rubbed her nose. "I wasn't looking where I was going, so it's my fault. No harm done."

She started to go around him, but he seemed inclined to talk. "You were humming. Good news?"

Whisper studied him. This was the dude who liked to drive his brother nuts and get him into trouble. Still, he was someone to talk to. She grinned. "Yes, my boss just told me that I don't have to work overtime anymore. That means I can go to school like I've been longing to do forever. I'm so excited."

"I see."

The twinkle of amusement in his eyes made her somehow wish Alec was there. She hated that feeling since it had no place in her heart. Thinking of Alec, she frowned. "I'm wondering if Alec had something to do with it because my boss mentioned his last name. There's no reason he would know, even though Alec came to pick me up last night." She was rambling. She clamped her lips together and pressed them tight.

Max's grin spread over his face. "Ah, my brother is becoming more protective of his mate." Max nodded as if it was all matter of fact. "He'll get worse before he gets better. Hopefully, he'll open his eyes to what's really happening before he pisses you off and you tell him where to go."

Okay, and now he's crazy again. She sighed. "I don't know what you're talking about. You said that mate stuff before. Alec is just wanting to date…well, a little more than that. I'm looking to date. He just wants sex."

She had no problem admitting the truth to his brother. With any luck, Max would repeat it to Alec, and it would give her a greater shield. A suspicion in her gut told her she was still fooling herself, but she ignored it.

Max leaned a shoulder against the wall and folded his arms over a broad chest. "Tell me. Was your boss getting a little too friendly with you?"

Her eyes widened. "How did you— I mean, what does that matter?"

He chuckled. "Instincts. You're his mate, so he will do whatever it takes to protect you, even stoop to the levels I've been known to use. My brother is for the most part straight-laced, but with a mate nearby, a man can lose his sanity."

Max's gaze grew cloudy, and she almost felt his pain. She rested a hand on his arm when he didn't appear to know she was there anymore. He shifted his shoulders and focused on her.

"My brother has never felt it, that sense of being with the right one. He's been with plenty of women over the years."

"Great to know. Thanks."

"No." Max lifted her chin when she turned away. "You are different."

"Oh, that's original. Listen, I'm not looking to get married, so don't even worry about it."

"It's deeper than that. I can't explain or he'd have my hide."

Max sighed and tweaked a lock of her hair. The touch was the affectionate kind a brother would give a sister, but they didn't know each other, so it seemed out of place. For some reason, she wondered where the leopard was. Would he deny they had one if she asked to come in and see it?

"Hey, girl."

Whisper froze when she heard Sheila's voice. They'd exchanged keys to each other's places in case of emergencies, but her friend used it as a reason to drop over whenever she wanted. Whisper almost never dropped in on Sheila simply because she didn't like it done to her. Even though she'd asked Sheila a million times to call first, her friend never took her seriously.

"Hey," Whisper responded and put space between her and Max, even though they hadn't been up to anything.

The moment she spotted Max, Sheila's eyes lit up, and she

forgot about Whisper. "Hello, there," she said to Max and sidled up to him.

Max towered over her shorter, much tinier friend. Sheila couldn't look more fragile or in need of male protection. In contrast, Whisper felt like a cow that could break his toes if she made one false move. Max didn't do more than nod, so she figured it was up to her to do the introductions.

"Max Macgregor, this is my friend, Sheila Tate. Sheila, Max is Alec's brother."

"Really?" Sheila cooed. "You're finer than your brother. I know people have told you that." She put her hand in Max's and waited as if she expected him to kiss it. Max held a half grin, but Whisper couldn't tell if he was attracted to Sheila or put off by her. He didn't kiss her hand but raised it to inhale at her pulse. Sheila giggled and simpered, making Whisper want to hurl on her. "I'm free for dinner tonight if you want to grab a bite."

Talk about eager. Whisper was beginning to think all Sheila's experiences with men weren't about how much hotter she was than Whisper, but rather how forward she was. Whisper didn't know why she'd never noticed before. The woman was over the top.

"Interesting," Max murmured. This time his expression went from amusement to open lust. He let his gaze explore at its leisure over Sheila's form, and her friend practically primped for his inspection. Whisper rolled her eyes.

"If you'll excuse me, I have to get going," she said. "Sheila, I'll catch you later, girl."

Neither of them answered her, so she strolled across the hall to her apartment and let herself in. She kicked the door closed with more force than necessary. She didn't know why the scene outside pissed her off so much. Max wasn't her man, and she wasn't interested in him in the least. He wasn't her type. As she stripped out of her work clothes she considered it. Maybe it was the fact that Sheila was so damn confident, and men always responded. After all, hadn't Alec when they were in the laundry room? He'd denied anything was going on, and she believed him for the most part. That didn't mean Sheila *couldn't* be seduce him, and that irked her. Sometimes she thought it was just a matter of time.

In her bra and panties, Whisper considered whether she wanted to take a shower now or wait until closer to bedtime. She glanced at her cell phone tossed on the bed and thought of Alec. She really wanted to see him, but it was too soon. Running into him in the hall instead of his brother would have been nice, but no, she had to keep a strong grip on her emotions. Lay low for a bit, and everything would be fine.

While she considered what else she might do—read or watch TV—a scratching at her balcony door caught her attention. She went to investigate and grinned when she saw the leopard. Without hesitation, she yanked the door open to let him in.

"You take a lot of risks, you nut. Someone could have seen you." She dropped to her knees when he was inside and scratched beneath his chin. "Hello, baby, how are you today?"

The cat purred under her caress, but then she paused. An odd sensation came over her. She had only seen Max the leopard a few times, and by no means did she think she knew every inflection of his beautiful, soft coat, but still, she was almost certain there was something different about him.

The leopard nuzzled its wide head into her cleavage, and she shoved him back with all her strength chuckling. "No, it's you. Still frisky, I see."

A frustrated mewl was the response, and then the cat seemed agitated, turning his head a little to the side as if to ask her a question. Whisper couldn't believe how humanlike he was. Maybe that's why Alec kept him as a pet.

"Oh, you're saying you don't remember licking my butt when you spent the night, huh? Well, keep that tongue in your mouth this time, big boy, or out you go. We won't tell Alec you stopped by if you leave early. Is it a deal?"

She stood and padded to the kitchen. Maybe she had a can of tuna she could feed the cat while she made dinner for herself. Having him there made her a little less lonely and the longing to see Alec a dull desire.

"Max, do you want tuna?" she asked him. The angry mewl made her glance over her shoulder from the cabinet where she was searching for his dinner. "What?"

He made another protest, and she shook her head.

"Alec gives you better food than that? What, do you eat at the table?"

In answer, the cat jumped up with lithe grace to a chair and sat down. She chuckled, and they sat in companionable silence throughout their dinner. Later, she came to the conclusion that Max the cat didn't like his name. He kind of growled at her whenever she used the name, so she dropped it with the intention of talking to Alec about a name change for his pet.

In her living room, she forewent pulling a blanket over her while she watched TV and allowed the cat again to jump up to join her. His thick fur warmed her legs, and he rested his wide head on her thigh. She tapped his nose when it ventured too close to her panties, and he settled down. Whisper scratched with absentmindedness behind his ears as she took in a couple of medical drama shows, her favorites.

When the shows were over, she flicked the TV off with the remote and settled back in her chair. A glance at the coffee table reminded her that she'd brought her cell phone in the room, and she chewed her lip. "What do you think about me seeing your owner? Will he break my heart?" she asked the cat.

Slanted green eyes blinked up at her.

"I know he thinks only of what his body wants and never considers the hurt of the other person. Women become attached to men when they sleep together. It's a bigger deal than just fulfilling the physical needs for us." She sighed and stared at the ceiling. "Do you know how many times I've gotten it wrong?"

The cat growled in protest. She laughed.

"Well not *that* many times. I don't dive into bed with every Tom, Dick, and Harry." The cat let out a puff of air, which tickled her pussy. She rolled away from him. "I can't bear being heartbroken again. I just don't want to. Maybe I'm closed off, and I can't take any man at face value anymore."

To her surprise tears welled in her eyes and slipped down her face. This was too soon to get all emotional. She'd only gone out with Alec once, but no one understood better than her how hopeful she'd get even with a few conversations. Right now, without any love involved, he could make her sad. How did they do it?

She sniffed and scrubbed at her face. The cat stood and jumped to the floor. He padded over to the exit, and she wiped away the water works the best she could. "Sorry for becoming a downer. You're ready to go? All right."

She opened the door and let him out, then returned to her bedroom. Ice cream would help, but she had none in the house. Even though it had grown late, she figured a trek to the convenience store was in order. She dressed and headed out. Maybe she should have turned Alec down. After all he couldn't know that the man she'd loved and was close to marrying had dumped her cold saying he'd fallen for someone else. The lover before that had been in a tragic accident, which took his right leg. After the accident, no matter how supportive she'd been, he drew further away until he didn't come around at all. The various guys she'd dated around those two weren't about anything. Sometimes she thought she was cursed, that all relationships with her were doomed to failure. Maybe it was true, and Alec should look out. No, he didn't want a relationship, so he was safe.

She headed out the door in a pair of jeans and a T-shirt. The store wasn't far, and the street was well-lit. At the corner, she stopped and waited for the light to change. The night might have grown late, but that didn't slow down city traffic. Everybody had somewhere to be no matter what the time.

"Excuse me, miss, you have the time?" A man had drawn up next to her in his car. Whisper raised an eyebrow. Was he serious? That was the oldest line in the book to start a conversation with a woman. Did he actually think she was going to talk to him this time of night?

"Nope," she replied and started to go around his vehicle.

"Come on, honey," he crooned. "Don't treat me this way. Let's talk a little."

"I'm in a hurry." Her clipped tone didn't seem to deter him. The man got out of the car and walked around to block her path. Whisper evaluated him. He was small but wiry. Although he didn't look like someone ready to rob her, that didn't mean he wasn't a bad guy. Making the wrong assumption could get her hurt or worse. Still, something told her he was just some idiot desperate for a girlfriend. "Get out of my way."

"How about this." He held out his hand. "I'm Kal. I have a job and as you can see a car. What's your name? Maybe we could—"

A snarl from the shadows caught both their attention. Whisper looked over her shoulder. All she needed to see was the glowing slanted eyes to know it was Alec's pet. She suppressed a smile and turned back to the guy.

"My boyfriend's dog"—A dog seemed more of a threat, and she didn't want to admit the animal was actually a leopard—"I wouldn't come any closer if I were you. My boyfriend trained him to devour any guys that try to hit on me."

Another low growl that was a great imitation of a dog if she said so herself did the convincing. The guy jumped back into his car and peeled out of there without looking back. Whisper burst out laughing. "Wow, you come in handy. Sorry about the dog thing, baby." She threw a kiss toward the spot where the cat had been, but she no longer saw his eyes or him. "You better get back home. I'll be fine now. Thanks."

The cat had lightened her mood, and she no longer needed the ice cream, but she went to pick it up anyway. Tomorrow or the next couple of days when she had her date with Alec, she might need it. Whisper didn't see the leopard, but something told her he wasn't far. She decided not to tell Alec about his pet protecting her just in case he wasn't allowed outside on his own, which she was sure he wasn't. How a wild leopard on the loose didn't attack people, she didn't know. The fact that he was smarter than the average cat was obvious, but she still should have her head examined for accepting it.

All was quiet back at the apartment, and Whisper put her ice cream in the freezer and then took herself off to bed. Tomorrow was another day.

Chapter Six

Alec rubbed a towel over his wet hair, frowning. What had he been thinking going to Whisper's apartment? He could admit in the privacy of his own thoughts that he'd longed to see her sooner than the three days she'd given him. He was a fool. Maybe he should cut this one loose before the situation got out of hand. Of course he didn't take Max's words seriously that she was his mate. Alec had never come across any woman that gave him that "feeling" so many of his kind talked about, and he refused to believe whatever draw Whisper held was anything other than a desire for her luscious body.

To deny excitement coursed through his veins at seeing her tonight and the thought of touching her was to lie to himself, and he wasn't in the habit of doing that. Another thing he wasn't in the habit of doing was going out onto the city streets in his leopard form. That was dangerous and foolish. They could not be discovered. Yet, when he heard her pass his place, he knew he would follow. The city wasn't safe for a woman alone at night, and he'd been proven correct when that bastard had tried coming onto her. Alec found himself using all of his willpower not to attack the guy. *If he had touched her...* No, that didn't bear thinking about.

He tossed the towel aside in anger and sat on the side of his bed. What the hell was this? In an instant, he'd gone from lusting for her to uttering possessive mewls like she belonged to him. The only knowledge that gave him any peace was that he wasn't behaving the way his brother had when he met Sarah. He'd been like a kitten in love, bouncy and playful whenever he was in her presence. Max had been intolerable at that time, almost sickening. Alec tolerated him only for

Sarah, who'd been a sweet woman, one of the best, and perfect for his brother. She'd been devoted to him.

Now that I think about it, I was almost jealous of him. I wanted what he had found. Well, until I came to my senses.

He put thoughts of Whisper and how much he wanted her out of his head for the time being. Tonight he would be a perfect gentleman. He'd show her a good time and then drop her at her door none the worse. His plan was to leave her wanting and unable to resist seeking him out. Then he'd welcome her with open arms.

Alec left his apartment and crossed the hall to Whisper's place. He'd had plenty of time to find a house now, but he was putting it off. The apartment was convenient. He could watch over her, and when he didn't Max did. For some reason antagonizing Alec by pretending an interest in Whisper had eased some of his brother's grief. Alec knew if Max thought she was his, he would not get in the way, so for now, Alec let him believe what he wanted. For the first time in months, Max wasn't driving him insane acting out the torment that was in his heart. If nothing else, Alec had to thank Whisper for that.

When Whisper opened the door, he did all he could not to let on how she affected him. Her beauty took his breath away. Wide brown eyes, soft thick lips, and a cute nose. She stood no higher than his collarbone, and although she was plump—which set his loins on fire— she still appeared fragile to him. He didn't appreciate the sense of wanting to protect her, but it was there inside of him.

"That dress," he breathed.

She frowned and looked down at herself. "You don't like it? I know it's a little clingy. I thought it wasn't so bad." She swung away from him a little trying to see behind her. He got a view of her curvy ass, and she was right, the dress was clingy. *Wonderfully* clingy. His palms itched for a squeeze, but he refrained.

"I love it. You look beautiful tonight, and blue is perfect with your smooth cocoa skin." He raised her hand, flipped it over, and kissed her palm. The tremble satisfied him that she was affected by his touch.

She blushed and lowered her lashes. Did she know the power she held in those eyes? He doubted it.

"Thanks," she murmured. "So why did I have to get dressed up? Where are we going?"

He tsked. "Wait and see."

When they reached the street, he watched for her reaction to the horse and carriage. Her eyes widened, and her mouth made a little O. He suppressed a smile. After he helped her into the carriage, Alec snapped the reins, and they were off.

"So cool. I've always wanted to take a carriage ride, but I never got around to trying it. No one I've ever dated wanted to try either." She set a hand on his forearm and squeezed gently. "Thanks, Alec."

"This is only the beginning of our date." He winked. "You can save your gratitude for later."

She rolled her eyes and pursed her lips. "Boy, don't even get excited. I am not rewarding you like that!"

He laughed. "I would never imply such a thing."

"Whatever."

The carriage took them through the park along lighted paths. He had to hand it to the city in keeping up with safety measures for its residents. Of course, nothing would happen to Whisper while he was at her side. He could guarantee it.

When the way opened to an area just off the path, Whisper leaned forward. "What is that?"

Alec said nothing. He let her discover the table and chairs, the soft music, a waiter preparing glasses of chilled wine. Alec helped her down from the carriage and couldn't resist a slight caress at her waist as he guided her to their table.

"Did you get special permission for this?"

He pulled out her chair and seated her. Bending over behind her, he spoke into her ear. "Don't worry. I want you to enjoy yourself."

While she still appeared nervous, her eyes did reflect enjoyment at the scene he had laid out before her. Two dozen roses and candlelight set the mood. Alec planned to take her into his arms after dinner to dance under the stars.

"Mm, this wine is delicious. Will you try to get me drunk?"

"Never," he answered. "I want you sober when I hold you."

She sucked her teeth but giggled.

The dinner progressed as he expected with them chatting. Alec kept conversation light about nothing in particular. He did discuss her relationship with her sister and why it was so strained, but when he saw her becoming upset, he steered it away to gentler topics. Something told him Whisper's sister considered her a failure and that the woman had little patience for her. He felt the offense. Even while he and Max had their differences and his brother pissed him off regularly, he couldn't imagine not running with his brother. They were close, and he had no doubt they always would be.

"So, do you dance?" he asked when they had finished eating for almost half an hour. Her eyebrows went up.

"Um?"

He extended a hand. "Come on."

"Where? Here?"

Again he felt the tremble, but she hid her nervousness well. The sweet smile got to him. He liked the crooked tooth at the topside of her pretty mouth. How he wanted to kiss her again, but he'd promised to behave himself. Already he'd broken their agreement about her selecting where she wanted to go. He had planned the entire evening without her input, so he would settle for holding her in his arms for the time being. Keeping his hands to himself didn't include what they were about to do, which was why he made sure they danced in the first place.

"Okay, fine, but don't get grabby." She laughed, and he joined her.

Alec pulled her against him. He thought she'd protest at the close proximity, but she didn't utter a word when her breasts pressed into him. Of course if she knew how hard she'd just made him, she might run. He shifted away to keep her from finding out and then rocked her to the beat of the music. At the same time, a breeze stirred her hair, and a tendril blew across her cheek. He brushed it away. She smiled her gratitude with an upturned chin. The invitation seemed clear, but he fought the impulse.

He whipped her away from him, guiding her movements with his hand in hers. He enjoyed the chance to watch her hips moving to the rhythm that only black women seemed to have, a hypnotic twist and dip that felt like his doom.

Her lips had been sweet that last time, and her body... *Does this woman know how sexy she is? How delicious she was in that thong?* He'd covered his desire with a smart remark, and he'd thought he made her hate him after that and her friend's actions. So it surprised him how easily she came when he held out his hand. She drifted into his embrace while he tried not to think she belonged there on a permanent basis.

No, Alec, this is about possessing her body, not her heart. That's all I want. She's not my mate. I have no mate and never will.

Alec spun her once again, and this time when he drew her, it was with her back to him. He let her feel what she did to him, and he grinned at her sharp intake of breath. One would think she was a virgin. No way a man had never enjoyed all of this. He peered over her shoulder and saw down the deep cleavage on display for him. Her breasts were a good size and would fill his palms. He wouldn't be a man if he didn't dream of sucking her nipples until they were rigid. Alec dipped his head and rested his mouth on the top of her head. He drew in a deep breath. She smelled amazing.

"You're...uh...enjoying the dance," she commented.

"Does it bother you?"

Her smile widened. "No."

Alec nuzzled her cheek and kissed it. Damn, he'd broken the rule, but she didn't protest. "Good."

When she raised her chin, he didn't resist going further. He captured it to hold her still while he claimed her mouth. Plundering the warm, wet interior was the only thing he could do as he splayed fingers over her belly. *Soft and so good.* He sucked her bottom lip between his and bit down just enough to startle but not hurt. She moaned in his mouth, driving him insane.

A roar rumbled to his throat when she moved out of his arms and walked back to the table. He stood where he was for a few moments, trying to pull himself together. At what point had the tables been turned and she began to seduce him?

He sat down at the table and smoothed his jacket front. "Would you like more wine?"

She held out her glass. "Please."

Alec obliged her in silence. His mind raced, and he searched it for conversation, something to get him back on firm footing and her into the palm of his hand.

"So why are you afraid of commitment?"

"Wha—?" His hand dipped, and red liquid stained the white tablecloth. Alec swore under his breath. Whisper laughed at him. Something harsh and arrogant trembled on his lips, but he bit it back. He didn't want to hurt her. In fact, looking into her eyes, he realized it would get to him to see pain there, worse if he caused it. *What the hell is the matter with you? Get it together. This is child's play.* "I'm not afraid of commitment. I've simply made a decision not to settle down."

She picked up a roll and began buttering it, not looking at him. For some reason, Alec needed to know what she was thinking. He hated that he didn't.

"A heartbreak can cause it or seeing your parents' failed relationship."

Nothing could have cooled his desire like their current conversation, and she'd done it on purpose. Of that he was sure. "My parents have a solid marriage, one built on respect and understanding."

Whisper glanced up, eyes wide. "Respect and understanding?"

He compressed his lips.

She patted his hand as if he were a child. "I've never seen two people more unalike as you and Max are."

He grunted. "Are you saying you like my brother better?"

"Oh don't be so touchy," she teased. "No, I'm not saying that at all. Just from what I've seen of Max, he's more open to loving. You said he'd just lost the love of his life, and he's grieving. You fight it like a wild animal."

She couldn't be closer to the truth, he thought. Still, he resented her insinuating that he was closed off. "Do I have to have a reason for choosing to live as I do? Why can't I just prefer it?" Alec heard the grumpiness in his tone, but couldn't stuff it down. The worse part of it was even while Whisper dug at him, he wanted her. He couldn't stop looking at her, breathing her in, listening to her voice. Maybe she was more of a seductress than her friend. Sheila was gauche, and that had always turned him off in a woman. Whisper was everything her friend was not. The table sat between them, and yet it wasn't enough. He needed her on his lap, moaning while he pleasured her with his hands between her legs. "I need to get you home."

"I thought—" She stopped, and the hurt he'd wanted to avoid surfaced in her gaze. "I'm too direct. I say the wrong things every time. I'm sorry."

Alec blinked in surprise when she suddenly jetted for the trees. He paused only a few seconds and then ran after her. "Whisper," he called.

Ahead, she made a sharp turn and left the path. He lost sight of her. The woman was fast on her feet, but that meant nothing. Even in his human form, he could pick up her scent. Whisper's natural fragrance teased his senses and felt like a seduction even when she wasn't trying. She called to him in her own way, and he followed with ease.

She stood, head down with her face in her palms. He thought at first she was crying, but she held herself very still. Maybe she fought tears. He walked up behind her and lay hands on her shoulders. She jumped a little but didn't pull away. Alec planted a kiss on the top of her head.

"I'm sorry," she said again.

"Don't be." He turned her into his arms and pulled her close. "I should be the one to apologize. I was a bear with you, and you didn't deserve that."

She glanced up at him in surprise, but he didn't give her a chance to speak a word. He covered her lips with his own, tasting that sweetness anew. Whisper didn't pull away, so he drew her closer and molded their bodies together. His body came alive with need. Had he wanted another woman as much as he wanted this one now?

The erection in his pants strained to be set free, and he found his hand exploring the side of her thigh to her hip and higher to her waist. When Whisper didn't stop him, he brought his hand around to stroke her breast. Through the thin material of her dress and bra, he felt the rigidity of her nipple, and it was his undoing. He craved much more. He wanted to taste more than just her delicious mouth.

The problem with dealing with humans was that his kind could be very aggressive when it came to sex. Not giving in to the instinct to slake their lust was a near impossible task. That was one of the reasons he never gave in to a relationship. No one woman had ever been enough for him, certainly not a human one, and he'd met few female shifters he could tolerate for more than a single night.

Alec pushed Whisper back against a tree, and she bumped it, expelling a soft breath. He followed with his body, pressing in tight. Without a second thought, he grabbed hold of the collar of her dress and tore downward. She cried out as the rending sound filled the quiet night. The swollen mounds straining against her bra took almost all of his attention before he forced his gaze higher to her eyes. Fear in the tawny depths stopped him. Shame washed over him. He had never and would never force a woman.

Alec fell back a step and dropped his hands to his sides. "I'm sorry. I shouldn't have done that."

He would have turned away and told her he would take her home, but she stumbled toward him. Alec had to close his eyes and swallow over and over when her breasts brushed his chest. Did the woman get what she did to him? A man could take only so much.

"Don't," she said.

He heard a rustle of clothing and opened his eyes. To his surprise, she'd drug her dress lower and tugged her bra straps over her shoulders to expose her nipples. They were puckered and dark like ripe berries. His mouth watered. "You don't know what you're doing, Whisper."

"I'm using my prerogative," she answered without hesitation.

Again he forced his gaze to meet hers. This time while there was nervousness, there was also determination. Her lips were set in a straight line, her jaw clenched and chin high. He hesitated, but then she raised one of his hands and laid it on her breast. A soft touch on his hardened cock put him beyond the point of no return.

"Let's just have some fun," she said.

He knew this wasn't what she preferred. Sex wasn't all fun for her. The act was more a physical expression of the love she felt for the right man. He knew all this, and shame washed through his mind before desire drowned it out. He couldn't say no.

Alec said nothing. Although her dress was ruined, he used the zipper at the back to loosen it some more and slipped it down her body to drop on the ground. She reached behind her to unhook her bra, and he caught her hands before she could follow with her panties. She stood there in nothing but her heeled shoes and her red panties. Her skin was smooth and brown. Her luscious figure rounded, breasts full and hips wide. He took in the sight of her thighs, thicker than any of his previous lovers, and he tormented himself with thoughts of them wrapped around his waist or parted while he delved between them with his tongue.

"Do you have any idea how beautiful you are?" he demanded.

She uttered a laugh that was half clipped, half trembling. "You don't have to say that. I've said yes."

"Foolish," he growled and dropped to his knees. She yelped when he ripped her panties to shreds and tossed the material away. Alec expected her cream to taste good, but he never imagined it would be this good. He pushed his tongue deep into her pussy and lapped at her juices. Whisper whined and shifted her hips. He caught them in a strong grip to keep her still while he feasted.

"Alec," she moaned in protest. He lapped faster, hungry for more. A tremor passed through her thighs, and he squeezed them as he pulled her closer. Alec came up higher to support her weight and let her legs rest on his shoulders. He ate her sweet pussy with relish, alternating between sucking at her clit and lips and delving inside her.

He hadn't been at it long before she cried out once again, and her limbs began shaking. A gush of cream rushed down her channel and filled his mouth. He moaned and massaged her little bud with his lips until the orgasm eased. After she was done, with his face bathed in her juices, he kissed his way up her belly and then stood up. Alec cleaned off and then undid his pants. He watched for her reaction to his erection. At nine inches, he knew he was a little too much for some women and just right for others. What was important in his opinion was that he knew how to use it.

Whisper's eyes widened when she saw his tool, and he grinned in satisfaction. She appeared more turned on than fearful, and he liked that. Once more, he parted her legs and aimed his cock toward her entrance. First, he teased her clit with the tip. Precome coated her bud which was still erect, but he pulled back.

"I need to cover up." She appeared alarmed at his words, but he chuckled. "Don't worry. I'm prepared." He peeled a condom from his wallet, tore into the packet, and had himself gloved within a matter of moments.

TWIN LEOPARDS – Tressie Lockwood

From the first entry, chills raced over his arms. She was so tight, he couldn't catch his breath. He leaned a hand on the tree behind her and paused. If he wasn't careful, he would come much too soon. So he seated his cock as deep as it would go and waited until he calmed down.

Whisper clutched his shoulders. Her eyes had drifted closed, and her lips parted. The panting told him she was just as affected by their intimate connection as he was.

"Just a moment, honey," he murmured.

"Yes."

Alec hoisted her up into his arms but kept himself buried to the hilt. He switched their positions so he could lean against the tree and support her weight.

"I'm too heavy," she protested.

"You're perfect."

He took his time withdrawing and then pushed hard and fast into her. She threw her head back and moaned. Alec took that as a sign that he should continue, and he let go. Pounding into Whisper, he let pleasure overtake him. His orgasm built, but he maintained control. With each thrust, he spoke into her ear.

"You like that, baby? You want more?"

"Yes, yes," she pleaded.

Alec complied. He pounded a steady rhythm, raising her up and allowing her to fall onto his cock. At the same time, he pushed in. The friction was out of this world, and it shook him from head to toe. He moved to kiss her lips, then her neck. His hunger built, and he had to lick and taste her skin in every spot he could reach.

Whisper called his name and dug her nails in his back. The pain added to the pleasure and drove him on. Her pussy clenched around his dick, milking it to the point that he couldn't hold on any longer. A growl rose in his throat, and he clamped his teeth together. With a heavy breath, expelled through his nostrils, he let loose. His come shot out into the condom, and he sagged against the tree in bliss.

Whisper whimpered as he let her legs down. At some point, she'd come out of her shoes, so she stood on tiptoe in the grass. She'd never looked cuter. He couldn't take his eyes off of her. "Are you tired?"

She'd been searching the ground, he imagined, for her clothing. When he spoke, she looked up at him, embarrassment plain. "No, are you?"

Alec grinned. "Not at all. If you can take me again, I'd like more. Maybe we could go to your apartment?"

She nodded.

Alec got her into her dress and shoes, and left the panties and bra. If she needed him to replace them, he would, but he couldn't wait to feel her under him in a bed. *Or maybe riding me.* At his errant thoughts, his cock began to grow again. He stuffed it away into his pants for the moment, and they hurried back home.

Alec couldn't get her stripped and prostrate before him fast enough. He gloved his cock and flipped Whisper onto her stomach. She squealed in delight. "You've got a big appetite."

"You don't know the half of it, honey."

With an arm around her middle, he hoisted her to her knees and drove into her juicy pussy. She cried out in pleasure, and he echoed it. Alec yanked her roughly back to his cock and watched as he pounded inside her. Just seeing his dick disappear into her sweetness drove him insane. He wouldn't get enough. Not all night if he could help it. He just hoped she could take him as many times as he needed to take her.

Chapter Seven

Whisper opened her eyes and shifted on the bed. Her head bumped something hard, and she muttered. Just as she forced her eyes opened, she remembered the night before. *Oh hell, what did I do?* Her blurred vision cleared to reveal Alec, asleep beside her. *Damn, damn, damn! Why?*

Why had she given in? Because she'd said the wrong thing and offended him? That was no reason to sleep with a man, damn it. He was a big boy. She moaned and scanned his body. The sheet she kept on the bed, along with the comforter was nowhere in sight. That allowed her a good view of Alec's form. Oh yeah, he was a big boy all right. There wasn't an inch of excess flesh on his hard body, and he was hung!

No amount of wine could erase the memory of how he'd taken her. Heck, with the number of times they'd done it the alcohol had plenty of time to wear off anyway. Still, she hadn't drunk much, so she couldn't blame anything but herself. Alec had given her the option of five dates. She could have turned him down and walked away. She could have kept him to his word. No, she'd let him tear her dress off in the woods and bang her brains out upside a tree.

"Goodness," she moaned. Just thinking about it turned her on again, but no, she regretted it. They'd moved too fast, and there was no way he'd respect her sleeping with him on the second date. No way in the world! "Why, why, why?"

"Are you okay?"

She jumped at the sound of his voice but didn't look up at him. "I'm fine. Thanks."

Sitting up, she discovered she was sore as hell between her legs. He had worn her out, but she'd had a million orgasms, or it seemed like it.

No, don't even think about it, Whisper. This is not going to happen again.

Her sheet was across the room near the door. How the heck had it gotten that far? Great, she'd have to get up and show him her big, wide butt in the light of day. She debated just staying there and waiting for him to get up instead.

"I think we both know last night shouldn't have happened," he said.

She froze.

"But we're adults, and..."

Whisper stopped listening. Now she knew he regretted what happened, too. Maybe he didn't enjoy it as much as he seemed to last night. Or maybe he thought she was going to get all clingy. Well, he was dead wrong.

"You got what you wanted. You can go." She stood up, ignoring her nakedness and walked across the room to the bathroom. Tears filled her eyes, but she blinked them away. "You don't have far to go, so I'm sure you can shower at your own place."

Wow, now that sounded cold. She hoped he'd think she was one of these modern women who thought nothing of sleeping with a guy when she chose to. Her previous denials and acting like she wanted to make him wait could be considered part of the game. He didn't have to know here she was again, having given in to the charm with no love—the one thing she wanted more than any other.

Rather than slam the door, she shut it quietly and turned on the shower. Only when she was under the spray did she let the tears fall. This time was the last she would let them go. Alec Macgregor wasn't worth any more than that. Last night was great. Yes, she was an adult, and now it was done. She wouldn't spare him another thought.

* * * *

Whisper didn't want to tell Sheila what happened, but she was her only friend, the only close person in her life, and she needed to talk it out. Having an ear to listen might make her hurt feelings lessen, and then she could get on with her life. The problem was thoughts of Alec consumed her. Every time she closed her eyes, she saw him behind her lids, stroking her, murmuring gentle words that would lead her to opening up to him. Even in her imagination, she felt the pull to be his. Her heart ached for his love. She just wanted to wave a magic wand and have all those emotions disappear.

"I have something to tell you," she said to Sheila a few nights after she'd slept with Alec. She stopped, hoping Sheila would do what she usually did—just keep chatting away about her latest lover. Her friend must have sensed something because she fell silent and turned to look at Whisper.

She squinted and studied Whisper. "Something's been up with you for the last couple of days."

"Just figuring that out?" Whisper muttered.

"What?"

"Nothing." She took a deep breath. "I slept with Alec."

"You did *what*?" Sheila shouted.

Whisper squirmed. She peered over her balcony where they were sitting and watched the people on the ground. A few had glanced up at Sheila's voice. "Keep your voice down, will you? Damn, I don't need the world in my business."

Her friend wasn't listening. From the expression on her face, she was fuming, although Whisper didn't see why. "I can't believe you did that. To go whoring—"

"Whoring? Excuse me? How is it whoring when I sleep with one guy, but it's having fun when it's you and…half a football team?"

Sheila rolled her eyes. "Now who's exaggerating? I dated three guys on the team."

"At the same time," Whisper reminded her. "And if you want to call it dating…"

"Anyway."

Her friend flopped back in her chair and put her feet up. They usually went to get their pedicures together, but Sheila had gone recently without her, not even asking Whisper if she wanted to go. That fact wouldn't have been a big deal if Sheila hadn't acted like she cheated on her when she'd done it once three years before. Sometimes their relationship made no sense to her, but she'd never bothered to analyze it or try to fix it.

"Anyway," Whisper repeated. "I did. A few nights ago."

"And?"

Sheila's attitude lacked the support she'd been hoping for. "Never mind. It happened. It won't again. I...I think I misjudged the kind of man he is. Or rather I judged it right and made a bad call."

"So he wasn't good in bed?"

Can't she see I'm hurt, and I need my friend? Damn!

"He was great in bed," she admitted. "*Really* great. Tell me about your latest."

She didn't have to ask twice. The anger faded from Sheila's eyes to be replaced by amusement. Whisper didn't have to do a thing other than make small noises like she was listening to the diatribe about how easy men were to manipulate. Apparently, she'd been absent when that training went on. They spent another half hour on the balcony until she figured out an excuse to get Sheila to leave. She just wasn't in the mood to talk or listen to how many men begged not to be cut loose. Of course that got her to wondering what Alec thought of her in bed. Had she been bad? Was he bored?

The week dragged by, and for the first time, Whisper wished she had overtime. Then she could bury herself under endless reports. School wasn't due to start yet, so that couldn't occupy her thoughts. She considered going to the library and then decided to get with the twenty-first century. She'd been thinking about buying a Kindle for a while. Now might be a good time.

Forty-five minutes later, she sat in the parking lot outside of her building fiddling with the electronic reader. The instructions indicated she needed to charge the device, but she'd gotten it to come on. Of course now she'd have to figure out how to buy books for it, but that might mean having an Internet connection.

"Ugh, complications."

Movement from the corner of her eye made her look up, and she spotted Alec strolling from the building. Her heartbeat kicked into high gear, and a sense of longing enveloped her. Whisper pinched her lips together and tried tamping the emotions down. At least she was parked in a shaded area on the other side of a van. Maybe he wouldn't see her before he reached his car, and she wouldn't have to face him. She felt like a coward for deciding to delay getting out of the car, but so what. No one knew except her.

She crouched a little lower and set her Kindle in the passenger seat. Alec reached the curb, and she worried he'd tumble over the edge if he didn't stop fiddling with his cell phone. As if he sensed its position, he stepped down without looking up.

While she watched, she noted the ripple in his thigh muscle, contracting to help him take each step. His jeans hugged his hips with perfection and outlined his crotch enough to make her mouth water. He'd paired the pants with a T-shirt that had been imprinted with a skull and feathers. She wondered if it meant anything. For some reason, it didn't appear to be the type of thing he would wear, but she didn't know him that well.

Probably why I shouldn't have slept with him, too.

He frowned and glanced up from his phone. Whisper realized she'd heard someone call his name. She stiffened when Sheila sashayed over. Whisper swore under her breath. Her friend had never been over this side of town so often.

Sheila stopped in front of Alec and laid a hand in the middle of his chest. She flipped her hair back and grinned at him while chatting. Alec had gone still, the look in his eyes fit to freeze hell. If Whisper had thought something was between them before, she stood corrected. No one could mistake the dislike Alec was exuding at that moment. Well, except for Sheila.

What pissed Whisper off though was that her supposed friend was still going after him. She couldn't shut the hell up for five seconds to let Whisper talk about what happened between her and Alec, and then she went behind Whisper's back and tried to get him—again!

How many times had it happened in the past? Sheila would claim she was just talking to the guys that were interested in Whisper, but she'd always been clingy with them. No man was off limits when it came to what Sheila Tate wanted, and that included Whisper's boyfriends. What the hell had she been thinking all these years to not recognize it for what it was and call Sheila on it?

Enough was enough. Whisper might not be dating Alec, but she'd made it clear they had at least something going on that she was trying to work through. Sheila should have respected that, but why would she? She never had before, and she wouldn't in the future.

No longer worried about avoiding Alec, she threw the car door open and stepped out. Alec was the first to notice her approach, but she didn't focus on him. She glared at Sheila, who was still too self-centered to stop talking.

"Sheila," Whisper called out when she was close enough.

The bitch turned and never once lost her game as her ass brushed Alec's thigh, and her fingers trailed his bicep. "Oh, hey, Whisper."

"*Oh, hey?*" Whisper echoed. "Are you for real?"

Sheila blinked at her. That was too much. Whisper stomped up to her and spared Alec a glance when she grabbed Sheila's arm.

"Excuse us. We need to talk." She all but dragged Sheila into the building and shut the door behind them. Her anger wouldn't allow her to wait until they reached her apartment for privacy. Hell, she didn't want Sheila in her place ever again. Whisper held out her hand. "Give me my key."

Still the woman was playing the innocent act. "What's wrong with you, girl? I was just talking to Alec. Why are you acting all threatened and everything? It's not like he's your boyfriend or that y'all have anything serious going on."

The crack across Sheila's cheek took Whisper by surprise even though she'd done it. "You have three seconds to give me the key to my place before I snatch your weave off. Five before I put you on the floor. Now I don't fight, but I guarantee you, I will win if we get into one today."

If Sheila's skin tone wasn't so brown, Whisper would have sworn the blood drained from her face. She dug into her purse and pulled out her set of keys. For a few minutes, she fumbled trying to get the key off the ring, and Whisper didn't bother offering to help.

"I've had it with you," she said instead. "You're the worst friend a woman could ever have. You think you're slick coming on to every man that has ever showed any interest in me. No. Every man *period*. You don't respect yourself. You sure don't respect me. You're selfish and only care about what you want and need. Well I'm done. You stay away from me. Don't even come within my air space, or I promise I will forget the kind of person I am and kick your ass all the way back to your place."

Sheila dropped the key in her palm. "You know jealousy—"

"Jealousy?" Whisper shouted and took a step forward.

Her ex-friend bolted for the door, flung it open, and almost ran down the walk to the street. A few seconds later, her little sports car started up—one that she'd gotten as a present from the football player she'd done—and peeled out of the parking lot. Whisper watched her go with regret and relief. Alec hadn't left yet. He seemed about to head her way with concern on his face, but she pivoted and darted up the stairs. She didn't want to face him. Hopefully, he didn't hear the argument. All she wanted to do now was take a pill to knock herself out and forget the world for a few hours.

Chapter Eight

"Why are you so grouchy lately?"

Alec pretended not to hear the question. He knew he'd been a hare trigger away from flying off the handle all week, but he wasn't discussing it with Max no matter how much his brother antagonized him. Max could read him like a book and vice versa, but he wasn't sharing his feelings if that was the man's aim. All that would get him is more of Max's stupid theory about Whisper being his mate. *Bah!* He didn't believe that ancient destiny stuff anyway. Sure, he could believe that Sarah was meant for Max, but then so could a lot of women have been—ones that were sweet-natured and who thought Max hung the moon. Of course he would fall in love. Well Alec Macgregor was not some romantic character who would fall prey to that type of stuff. He could use it to hook a woman into giving him what they both wanted, but he didn't buy into the myth anymore than the next logical man. Whisper Price was just another beautiful woman. Sure, he would have liked to have her in his bed a while longer, but it didn't matter. Someone else would take her place soon enough.

As soon as I bother going out to meet a new one.

He had been lying at the apartment, barking at every sound Max made and refusing to close on his new house. There was no reason why he was still here, none why she should still occupy his thoughts at every waking moment. Hell, every sleeping moment, too. Why? She was...

She is excellent in bed. Sensual, beautiful, innocent, and experienced all rolled into one. I want to touch her and kiss her. I want to taste her sweetness and hear her cries of ecstasy.

He could dismiss it as just a strong physical attraction if it ended there, but he missed her laughter, too. He had considered telling her about his book and getting her opinion of it. That was crazy in itself. When he realized she'd argued with her friend and thought it might have something to do with him, he was going to talk to her and assure her he had no interest in Sheila. Whisper had run from him, and he hated acknowledging even to himself that it hurt.

"I'm not grouchy," he shouted, taking Max by surprise since he'd waited so long to answer.

"Okay, I'm convinced."

The obvious sarcasm made him scowl at his brother. "Just leave me alone. I'm having a bad week. It happens."

His brother shrugged. "Sure, to men who deny themselves their mate."

"Don't start, Max."

"Just saying."

Alec surged to his feet and headed toward the balcony. The apartment felt too small. They weren't used to such enclosed spaces. All of his family enjoyed large houses and acres of land around it for running in their animal form. He didn't know what he'd been thinking moving here. The sooner he relocated the better. He'd intended to allow Max to stay at his house as long as his brother needed him, but Max seemed a lot livelier. *He's finding new enjoyment in life by tormenting me.* Maybe he would suggest his brother start looking for his own house if he intended to stay in the area.

At the balcony door, he turned, "Whether you believe she's my mate or not, I'm not going to see her again. In the end, we can choose whom we want to be with, and I choose to continue the way I always have. If you don't like that, well, that's your problem."

Max made no more comments, and for that Alec was grateful. Even as he said the words, he didn't wholly believe them. Whisper occupied his thoughts more than he liked. He tried shutting her out and not bringing that sweet face to mind, but it remained impossible. Maybe if he got out of here after the sun went down, he could run in his leopard form until exhaustion took hold. Then when he hit his bed, he'd sleep and not dream of her. One could only hope.

Waiting through the rest of the day proved to be torture itself. Alec spent a few hours on his book, but everything he put on paper sounded hollow and unemotional. He felt like he lost his creativity, which frustrated him all the more. The night couldn't come soon enough, and with it an overcast sky. He didn't care. Running wouldn't take thinking. He could give in to his instincts, hunt a little, and forget about her even if for a short while.

Rather than take his car, Alec walked to the wooded area where he would take his run. When the trees hid him from public view, he removed his clothes and left them where they wouldn't be found. Then he shifted and took to all fours, pounding the ground beneath his paws. A growl rose up in his throat and instead of suppressing it like he would have around humans, he let it build and explode from his lungs in a full on roar. The burden of staying hidden and controlling his animal nature began to lift. He ran faster, his muscles burning, breath coming in heavy pants.

The ache for Whisper didn't release him as he'd thought it would. She wasn't in the forefront of his mind, but he felt her there, always present, almost as if she was a part of him. That was ridiculous. She was human, and his kind didn't connect in such a way with those who weren't like him. Sarah had been a shifter, a cougar. She wasn't rare, but she was special. If Alec even thought of finding a mate, he'd choose his own kind.

Stop! he shouted in his mind. *Enough of thinking along these lines. Just run.*

He let everything go—his irritation at Max, his fear of not being good enough with his writing, and Whisper. The sounds of nature, its scent, only that consumed him, and he pressed on for hours. By the time he decided he'd outrun his demons, the sky had opened up. Alec was soaked when he walked back to his clothes in the form of a man. He dressed and headed home.

Before he reached the parking lot, he smelled her in spite of the dampness in the air. All that he had accomplished in reaching a state of peace washed away with one glimpse of her. She stood at her car leaning in. When she straightened with something in her hand, the night-lights bathed her beautiful face, and he went still staring at her.

He wasn't too far away to see water hanging from her long lashes or the lock of hair plastered to her cheek. Why had she come out in the rain at night? He watched her protect what looked like a book or a journal under her top, but that only led his gaze to her full breasts, highlighted by her damp T-shirt. *Damn it, Whisper, can't you have mercy on a man?*

She looked up as if he'd spoken out loud, and their gazes met. Alec had no intention of turning away. He couldn't have if he tried. Some force drew him in her direction. He thought at first that she would run again as she'd done before, and he didn't think he could stand it if she did. Whisper stayed put until he was a few steps away, and then she turned her back to him. His heart seemed to stop, but she peered over her shoulder at him. *An invitation to follow.*

He didn't question it but fell into step behind her. They headed into the building and up the stairs. At her door, she paused. He hesitated nearer to his, but again she met his gaze, with hers so full of doubt. She disappeared inside. He waited a moment longer, and when the door didn't shut, he slipped into her place.

Her hands fluttered at her sides where she stood a few steps away from him. "I'll get you a towel."

Alec would have told her he was fine, but she was already gone. He moved into the living room and found a spot on the carpet rather than mess up her furniture. Whisper reappeared carrying a thick red towel and handed it to him. With another, she dried her hair. To his disappointment, she'd changed into a dry T-shirt. That didn't stop him from admiring her figure though. She was still beautiful.

"Thanks." He dried his face and rubbed the towel over his hair. "Why were you out there in the rain? What was that book?"

She grinned, and he realized there had been strain in her face. He hated that he might have been the cause of it. "That wasn't a book. Well not exactly. It's my new Kindle. I'm trying an e-reader for the first time, and I'm excited. Have you heard of it?"

He nodded. "Yes, I own a few, one of which is a Kindle."

"Aw." She pouted. "So I'm Johnny Come Lately."

Damn, her lips were kissable. He forced his gaze away from them and focused on the device she'd picked up from the table. "You'll like it. I devour probably a dozen books a month with mine and have an extensive library."

Her eyebrows went up. "Really? I'm impressed."

He chuckled. "Meaning you thought I was an illiterate Neanderthal?"

She giggled. "You said it. Not me."

They chatted about their likes and dislikes in the world of books. Alec threw out a few author names that were his favorites and found that she'd heard of each one, but read two. Her interests weren't the same as his as far as genre. Whisper enjoyed paranormal and shifter stories, some fantasy. He loved mysteries and thrillers. Of course, he couldn't help the swell of pride knowing she was into books with his kind being the central characters. He had avoided reading them, figuring they would be absurd and more offensive to their true nature than anything else.

"I write." He threw the words out while feigning an interest in the pictures on the wall. They were generic at best. Now that he'd said it, his stomach cramped. He was ashamed of his weakness and the small hope that she would be impressed with this as well. While she remained silent—and how long did it take for the woman to respond for cripes sake?—he argued with his decision to say anything. If there was anyone he should have confessed to, it should have been Max. However, Max wasn't the reading type. He liked to get out and live life, not get it from a book. Not that Alec didn't. *Damn it, man, get a grip on yourself. She doesn't care, and it doesn't matter.*

"Wait, did you say you write? Like in an author?" The awe was plain in her tone. "Oh wow, I've never known a real author personally." She rolled her eyes. "Well, a couple people I work with have written books on trading, but yawn! What's your genre? Can I read one of your books?"

As she scooted closer to him, excitement on her face, he held up his hands and laughed. He couldn't have hoped for a better reaction. Pride swelled inside him, but he resisted running home to get his laptop to show her a sample. "I'm not that far down the line yet. I'm in the process of writing a thriller. I'm halfway through."

"That's so awesome." He saw sincerity in her eyes. "Can I read it when you're done? What's it about?"

Alec hesitated for just a few seconds. This was what he wanted, someone to share his love of reading and his passion for writing. He couldn't be a wimp about it. That was definitely not in his nature.

His comfort level rose as he shared the details of his story with her. Alec lost himself in the way she sat at rapt attention, eyes wide, lips parted as if she couldn't wait to hear what came next. The killer's motives, his methods, Alec intended to keep to himself, but she dug out every detail, asking questions that let him know she was not ignorant.

"He leads her to the seaside, to the old house where he grew up," Alec explained.

"Why when he could just as well have done it at her father's shop?" Whisper countered. "I mean, that place held significance in his humiliation and pain, too."

Alec laughed, and before he knew what he was going to do, he laid a hand alongside her face. Her skin was baby soft, so smooth, and this close he picked up her scent. She smelled of roses and raindrops. "Your mind is like lightning."

She went still, and he snatched his hand away. When had she come so near? He fought the temptation to pull her onto his lap and stood up.

"I should probably go."

He moved toward the door, and she stood and followed. He expected her to say something, but she remained silent. Alec's entire being wanted to turn and take her into his arms, and his muscles ached as if they contracted to keep him from doing it.

At the door, she stopped him with a hand over his. The contact sent electric currents up his arm and down into his groin.

"I meant what I said," she said in a low tone. "Your ideas are incredible. I bet your book will be a success, and I would love to read it."

"Even though I told you the entire plot start to finish?"

"Definitely."

She smiled up at him. He curled his fingers into his palm.

"Okay, then I'll bring it by tomorrow." He said it with as little emotion as possible, but he didn't look away from her or move.

Alec made no conscious decision to do it, but the next instant he had her on the door, legs spread and wrapped around his waist while he devoured her mouth. The protest he expected sounded more like a moan of delight, and Whisper's hands crawled up his arms to lock behind his head. She opened to him, welcoming his tongue. Alec hoisted her higher, squeezing her ass as he kissed her.

"Damn it, you taste good, baby," he muttered against her mouth. "More, give me all of you."

"Yes," she moaned.

He didn't need any more invitation than that. Alec allowed her feet to touch the floor long enough for him to rip her clothing from her body. He yanked her T-shirt over her head and paused when her luscious breasts came into view. He thumped a hand on the door and pressed in closer.

"I need to be in you."

She trembled, and even that turned him on. When she went to unbutton his pants, he let her do it, watching with interest. She took his hard cock into her hands, but he wasn't about to let her go down on him. Not now. He'd spoken the truth when he said he had to get inside her. His sense of smell, already very strong, was overwhelmed with the scent of her cream. She was wet. He didn't need to feel it to know it ran thick down to the tops of her thighs.

Alec shoved his pants over his hips along with his boxers, and then picked her up. Her weight didn't strain his muscles in the least. In fact, he got off on all her curves, the color of her brown skin, the smoothness. *And oh the feel...* He sighed when his cock slid into her channel. Moist yet tight, it stretched around his girth, making him have to work to get himself all the way in.

"Damn it, baby, how can you still be so snug? You're going to make me come."

"I'm sorry."

He stroked her cheek. "No, don't be sorry. You feel incredible. Your body is perfect."

"You're bigger."

He stopped mid-thrust. "What do you mean?"

She'd shut her eyes and clung to his shoulders as if the sensations were a bit too much. Her heartbeat pounded in his ears, and her breaths had picked up speed. She moaned and nuzzled her face into his neck. When she spoke, her lips were on his pulse. The vibrations almost moved him to an orgasm even though he had stilled.

"You're bigger than last time, like you're more turned on. I thought you were giant then."

He drew back a little. "Am I hurting you?"

"Hell, no. If you take it out now, I'm going to kill you."

Alec chuckled. "Then by all means, let me please you, my sexy goddess."

Her lips tightened at his pet name, and something told him she didn't like it. That made him laugh all the more until she began to wiggle her hips. He was gone. Alec got his cock seated all the way inside her and then began moving at a steady, if slow pace. He picked up speed and thrust faster. Before long, he pounded into her, his desire driven higher with each grind and the noise of their coming together. Whisper was right. He was harder because he was turned on more than he'd ever been before. She filled his senses, drove him insane. He couldn't get enough—not in this lifetime. Maybe when he'd come, he'd feel more in control. He only hoped so.

Whisper cried out his name. Her head dropped back, and she whimpered. Alec feasted his eyes on her sweet face, her swanlike neck. He bent to run the tip of his tongue along the graceful column and thrilled in the tremor that passed over Whisper.

"I'm going to..." she said on a rasp. "I need to..."

She couldn't seem to finish the words. He didn't care if she did or didn't. Knowing what she meant and that he'd brought her to the brink took him higher. Alec's balls tightened and rose. He clenched his jaw and dropped his forehead toward her throat. The muscles in his core convulsed and contracted. One word eeked past his lips—her name. He let go on a last plunge into her wet pussy, and held himself there. Whisper mewled so sweetly, he crushed her to his chest. They came together in a way he couldn't have choreographed if he tried.

When they were done, Alec backed up a step. He raised Whisper off of his shaft and set her on her feet. She swayed, and he held on until she got her bearings. Now that his lust had been satisfied, reason returned. He left her standing at the door and took two big strides back to put space between them.

Whisper, too, seemed to come to her senses. She flitted on tiptoe to her discarded clothes and put them on. "I—" she said but didn't continue.

Why had he come here? He was only encouraging her. He knew

women, and they drew conclusions at this kind of thing. If she thought he couldn't resist her, she would begin to believe there was more to his feelings. He refused to use her for her body and allow her to read something warmer from it.

"I should go," he said.

Although he could sense fear, being a leopard shifter, he couldn't read other emotions unless he saw the signs in expressions or body language. He didn't need to look at Whisper to know his words hurt her. Like a knife turned in his gut, he hated himself for doing that to her. He should have been stronger and not come here tonight. This was his fault. *Damn it, I know better than this, and I don't make these kinds of mistakes anymore.*

He took a step in her direction. "Whisper—"

She flinched at his use of her name but waved her hand without looking at him. "You're right. You should go."

He opened his mouth to speak again.

"Go!"

He nodded although she wasn't looking at him. He left the apartment, and closed the door behind him.

Chapter Nine

Alec stood at the counter and received the beer the bartender handed him. He took a sip and then turned to survey the crowd. On a late Friday night, the place was packed wall to wall, and there were plenty of women who peaked his interest. Well, they would have peaked his interest a month ago, or even a couple of weeks. Before his mind was consumed with thoughts of Whisper, and his body craved to touch hers. He'd come here tonight to find someone—*anyone*—who could take away the insanity that Whisper brought.

A couple days ago, he'd given her his manuscript. For a good hour, he had argued with himself to forget it, and he'd told himself her opinion didn't matter. Besides, after their parting in her apartment, she wouldn't be interested anyway. He'd lost the battle, and after spending hours getting more of the story on paper and out of his head, he'd packaged it up and left it at her door. Later, when he returned from a few errands, he found the envelope gone, so he could only conclude that she got it. For all he knew, she might have tossed it into the trash when she realized what it was. So here he was looking to remove the obsession he had for the woman.

A blond at the other end of the counter smiled when she caught his eye. He nodded but kept his gaze moving. She was beautiful, but his crotch didn't stir at her dress's plunging neckline. For an instant, he paused on a black woman. As far as he could see she was one of only two in the bar that night. The rest of the women were white. He considered approaching her. Maybe another black woman could erase Whisper. A feeling of revulsion washed over him. No. The only mocha beauty he wanted from here on was Whisper. He didn't want to admit it, but it was true nonetheless. He would deny himself the pleasure of her, but he wouldn't seek it in another woman like her. No, the farthest was best.

With this in mind, he scanned the place again and focused on a petite brunette near the entrance. He made his way through the crowd and drew up to her. When he leaned in close, it felt like he bent from miles away to her short stature. "Buy you a drink?"

What he wanted to say was "let's go back to your place" and dispense with pleasantries, but that would be insensitive, and while he didn't want to get into a relationship, he didn't want to hurt anyone either. Least of all Whisper. Realizing he was thinking about her again, he clenched his jaw, tightened the hold he had on his beer, and forced himself to focus on the woman in front of him.

She offered a half smile and flipped her hair over her shoulder. He read the flurry of emotions over her face like a book. She considered whether to play hard to get or to let him know she was open to what he really meant. This particular bar didn't have a lot of dancing going on, and the place was too loud for any meaningful conversation. Therefore, pretty much everyone here was looking for a hookup.

"Sure, baby." She laid a hand over his. "I'll have what you're having."

Her bold move of taking his drink from his hand and raising it to her lips to take a swallow had turned him on in other women before. Tonight his emotions fell flat. In fact, he was beginning to worry that his cock wouldn't get hard at all. That had never happened.

He moved behind her and brought his mouth close to her ear. "I'm Alec. What's your name?"

She murmured something he didn't hear. He couldn't stir enough curiosity to ask what she said, but her physical reaction told him all he needed to know. She practically purred and brushed her ass to his thigh. Alec held still where he was. In the past, he would have placed a light palm at her waist and assessed things further. Some wanted a little more petting before they gave in to what they both wanted. He wasn't in the mood to play the game but kept the expression of interest firmly in place.

The brunette turned to face him and rested her hands on his chest, head tilted back, lips parted. "Take me home?"

He almost sighed in relief. "Of course."

They left the club in a hurry, and he drove the three miles to the address she gave him at record speed. Before long they were out of the car and in the house, shedding clothes and kissing. *She's holding her lips too tight. She's too damn short. Come on, damn it. Get hard. There, some life!*

He battled to calm his mind and stop being critical of her. This wasn't like him. He could teach any woman to be a better lover. He'd carefully paid attention to them over the years to learn how to please them as well. The brunette had placed his hand on her breast, which was a good size. By now his cock should have been rock solid. Hell, it would have been with just a few words between them at the club, but right now it was semi-alive. He cursed himself. *And damn Whisper! Get out of my head.*

In a burst of determination, he bent and lifted the brunette into his arms. She shrieked in delight, and he carried her down the hall of her apartment. She directed him to the back bedroom, and he kicked the door wider. Alec dumped her on the bed and followed her down, pinning her small figure to the mattress. Slender bones poked him in the groin. He grunted.

"Oh, baby, I'm hot for you, too," she teased, mistaking his grunt for excitement. Alec suppressed a laugh. This was not a humorous situation. Or maybe it was.

When he leaned up to raise her dress higher on her hips, running a hand along her thigh, a ding made him stop. He realized it was his phone and sat up. That was a text message, and Max knew better than to bug him right now since he'd known where Alec was going tonight. Max had nagged him not to go the entire time he was getting dressed.

Not until Alec had called him an old woman did his brother stop.

"Hold on a second," he told the brunette. He couldn't bring himself to use endearments, something he would have done at any other time. The display read Whisper's name. He hadn't erased her from his phone. His chest tightened, and yet, his heart rate sped up.

"I finished it," she wrote. *"It was unbelievable, and I can't wait to see what happens next. We can talk about it whenever you have a chance… If you want."*

Alec's hand spasmed on the phone. He tried suppressing the excitement rising inside, but it wasn't to be denied. Not even glancing at the woman on the bed, he dialed Whisper. She answered on the second ring.

"Don't say you liked it if you didn't. I know it has flaws."

"Don't be stupid," she countered and laughed. "You can't be so blind you don't see that you're brilliant. I mean I was chewing my nails all the way through."

He smiled at her words but tried to keep his cool. "I'm glad to hear it. And the one scene we discussed? What did you think of that? I think I explained better why he chose the old house where he grew up."

"Oh my goodness, yes," she exclaimed. "It all came clear when I read further."

He was about to respond when the brunette sat up on the bed and slammed a fist on the mattress. "What is your problem, Alec? Do you want to fuck me or sit on the phone all night?"

Alec froze and then glared at her. The way she flinched he knew he got his point across to shut her mouth. He turned back to his phone. "Whisper?"

She didn't answer, but she was still there because he could hear her breathing.

"Whisper, listen…" He stopped. What was he going to say? They weren't together, but he still felt like he'd just betrayed her. He could only imagine how hurt she must be. "Honey, I—"

"Just leave the rest of it outside my door just like you did this one," she interrupted in a rush. "I'll repackage this and leave it with Max if he's home. If not, it'll be in front the door when you get back. Bye."

She hung up. Alec swore. The brunette kneeled behind him and put a hand on his shoulder. He shoved it off and stood up. "Sorry. Something's come up."

He gave no other explanation but dressed and left without another look at the woman. The night was shot, and there was no way he was going to get into it—especially when what he wanted more was to wring that damn woman's neck for yelling out like that. Still, this was his fault. He never should have called Whisper. He never should have given her the book. They'd made another break, and that's where it should have stayed. Now, there was no question she wouldn't speak to him again, and that was the way it should be.

* * * *

"Hey."

Whisper started and turned around. She'd thought it was Alec at first, but then she realized the voice had a slightly different inflection. That meant it was Max. Still, she didn't feel like seeing him either. His face, so like his brother's, tormented her and made her ache to see Alec. *Stupid woman, even after you caught him moving on like five seconds after we were together.*

She couldn't pin down when it happened, but she was connected to the man on an emotional level, and she never meant it to be that way. They had been on two dates for Pete's sake and had sex twice. After the other night, there was no way they were sticking to the five date deal. She had no intention of speaking to him again. In fact, when she got the last of his book and had read it, she planned to write up a report of her thoughts and leave it at that. Then he could have sex with as many women as he chose. The lump in her throat and the wetness on her lashes would go away after a while.

"What do you want, Max?" She had come to the park to get away from everything and enjoy the fresh air and quiet. If she'd known Max would be around, she'd have chosen the mall. Not likely those two would be there. Then again, she'd forgotten Max's love of being in the buff out here. Thinking that, she eyed him from head to toe. He wore a T-shirt and shorts that showed off his muscular well-toned legs. She sighed.

Max grinned like he knew what she was thinking. "What are you doing out here alone? A beautiful woman like yourself should be beating off the men and making my brother jealous."

She rolled her eyes. "Please. Me and Alec are not a couple. I don't care if he gets jealous or not."

"Don't you?"

She glared at him.

Max took the bench space beside her. She resisted getting up and walking off. No matter how much the man annoyed her, she didn't want to hurt his feelings. That was stupid, because it didn't seem that men like them would be easily hurt. Not Alec anyway.

"You're his mate, Whisper," Max said. "Whether he wants to admit it to himself or you have no understanding of what our kind are like, it's still true."

"Your kind?" She folded her arms over her chest and crossed her legs. That made her look down at them and wonder how much more weight she had to gain before she couldn't do it anymore. "The crazy kind?"

So much for not hurting his feelings.

Max laughed. "I admit I'm a little off the beaten path in the way I approach things, but I like to think I'm fun."

She didn't comment.

"I mean leopard shifter," he explained.

Whisper blinked.

Max sat forward. He leaned his elbows on his thighs and laced the fingers of both hands together. When he looked at her, his expression showed his earnestness for her to understand. For some reason she wanted to get it, to not think this dude was off his rocker. Max didn't scare her. Maybe it was because Alec had told her about his girlfriend dying. If she'd found the right one and loved him with everything inside of her, wouldn't she be a little off for a while if he died?

"I have no problem telling you the truth about us," Max went on, "because I *know* what you are. There's not a doubt in my mind, and none of us has ever denied our mate. Leave it to my brother to screw that up though. Alec always did things his way."

"Funny, that's the impression I get of you." She pursed her lips and met his gaze without wavering. Max only grinned.

"Then my brother and I are alike more than he admits." He stood up and paced in front of her. "Alec isn't that social. He doesn't go in for family functions, what we call gatherings. They don't happen often, of course, but he hates them. Everyone acts like our entire existence is supposed to be taken up with finding our mate and settling down to have cubs."

Whisper wrinkled her brow at him. "Cubs?"

He sighed. "I'm not doing a good job of explaining, am I?"

"Not really. No." She stood up, ready to leave. "Look, it doesn't matter to me, okay? Do what you want to do. Alec can kiss…well, he can live his life any way he wants. It has nothing to do with me. I don't want to talk about him anymore. And since I'm not going to be dating him, there's really no reason you and I should be friends. I hope you understand. Have a nice day."

She started past him, but Max grasped her hand. She tried pulling away, but the pressure increased. The first touch of alarm hit her. Maybe Max was crazier than she thought, and she shouldn't have dismissed it as him just being depressed at his loss.

"I'm sorry, honey," Max said in a low, controlled tone. His gaze when he met hers was so intense that she shivered. Still, a little of his humor shimmered behind it, and she tried holding onto that to calm down. "My brother is a fool, but I'm not going to let him lose this one chance."

"W-What do you mean?"

All she saw was his other hand come up, and then all went black.

* * * *

Whisper opened her eyes and squinted. The décor of the room she was in wasn't familiar, but the structure was. She recognized the slant of the roof near the window. In her apartment, the slant was on the opposite side of it. Her chest hurt as her heart seemed to want to jump out of it. Less light came in through the blinds indicating time had passed. Memory of Max doing something came back to her, and as soon as she recalled, the door opened, and he stood in it, arms folded over his chest and smiling.

"What the hell do you think you're doing, Max?" To her annoyance, her voice shook a little.

The smile disappeared from his face, and his brows creased in concern. "Don't be afraid, Whisper. I promise I'm not going to hurt you. This is just to get things going in the right direction."

"What is?" she demanded.

He raised his hands in a calming motion. "Easy. All in good time. Soon my brother will come back, and then it's show time. However, we have to get you ready."

She resisted cowering on the bed and instead looked around for a weapon as he approached. Max chuckled.

"You're feisty, so perfect for him." He sat down on the side of the bed. Whisper swung at him with all her might, but he caught her wrist with ease. He brought her hand to his lips to kiss, but she jerked away.

"I can't believe you did this. Did losing your girlfriend send you this far over the edge?" She regretted it as soon as the words were out of her mouth, but Max went very still. His eyes glazed, and the flash of pain she caught went straight to her own heart. "I'm sorry."

He appeared to force a shrug. "It's fine. Now about you..." He reached for a glass at the side of the bed, which she hadn't noticed before. "You're probably thirsty after your ordeal."

She rolled her eyes and snatched the glass from him. "Don't change the subject. What are you planning? I know you think you're doing the right thing for me and Alec, but what I'm trying to get through your thick head is that there *is* no me and him."

She was thirsty, so she drained the glass and got back to glaring at him. Max remained silent watching her, and that's when she figured out he'd drugged the juice.

"Damn it," she murmured. Something like melted butter descended over her head. The sensation was so strong, she wanted to reach up and touch her hair to see if it wasn't just her imagination. "Max, don't..."

He stroked her cheek. "Like I said, I promise I won't hurt you. Contrary to what it seems like I love my brother very much. I'd die for him."

"You will die when I'm not drugged, because I'm going to kick your ass."

He chuckled. "I like you. Too bad you weren't for me." He guided her to lie down against the pillows and pulled a comforter over her. Whisper found it hard to struggle out of his grasp. "My plan is to make him think we're having an affair. He'll be pissed off and fight for you."

She blinked a few times trying to focus. "That's dumb."

He laughed again. "Why?"

"Because he's not going to fight for me. He's more likely to think I'm a dirty slut, sleeping with him first and then his brother. He'll want nothing more to do with me. Not that he does now anyway." She turned her head and stared toward the window. She wouldn't cry over Alec.

Max kissed her forehead. "My brother must have hurt you. Just think how much punishment it will be for him thinking we're having sex."

Her attention flew to Max. "We're not having sex!"

"No." He sighed as if he regretted it. "You do have a nice ass. Taste good, too."

"You've never—"

"My sweet Whisper, do you remember Max the cat licking your ass?"

A shriek erupted before she could hold it back. "Stop playing games. That's impossible. I always knew the two of you were crazy. I should never have gotten involved with you or Alec."

"It was meant to be."

"Stop saying that!"

He didn't answer but reached beneath the covers and began pulling her T-shirt up. Whisper slapped at his hands, but her strength had decreased big time. She might as well be a little kitten for all the effect she had on pushing him away. Before long, he'd taken off every stitch of her clothing, including her panties. The only consolation was that he hadn't looked beneath the comforter, and he'd been careful not to allow his hands to touch her skin too much.

Whisper clutched the cover to her chest when Max stood up. She searched her mind for some way to change his. "If what you're saying is true about how Alec feels about me, then he'll be pissed."

He nodded. "I'm counting on it. He knows the kind of woman you are, that you're not a whore. He'll want to protect you from me."

"That's what I'm saying. He'll kill you, Max. Think about what you're doing."

"I've thought about it." He pulled his shirt over his head and tossed it aside. Whisper's stomach clenched with nerves. "Do you think I have much to live for anyway? My mate is gone."

Her heart constricted. "Oh, Max."

"Don't worry over me. You'll find happiness with my brother soon enough, and maybe have some kids. I won't matter." He sat down on the bed again. Whisper suppressed a yawn, bringing her hand up to her mouth. Max stroked her hair. "Almost."

The drowsiness was taking more of a hold. She could barely keep her eyes open and forced herself to talk. "S-So this cat shifting delusion…"

"It's not a delusion, sweetheart."

She let her lids shut but continued the conversation. "Can you prove it?"

"I could."

The damn stroking was adding to her tiredness. When his voice came again, it was from somewhere closer. She felt the bed dip down and cried out. He soothed her with soft words.

"Alec will prove it to you. That's his right to show you, and I won't take it from him." Another gentle kiss to her forehead. "He's coming."

Whisper didn't hear anything at first, but a few seconds later, a door opened somewhere else in the apartment. Whisper wanted to protest, but she no longer had the energy to speak. Max shifted on the bed, and it felt like he leaned over her. A heavy leg was slung across hers. He moaned rather loud and murmured, "Oh, baby, you feel so good."

If she was alert she'd have thought it sounded lame and he wouldn't win any Oscars with his performance, but it was more than enough for Alec. The door opened and smashed against the wall. Whisper drew in a sharp breath. From the explosion of sound he had to have ripped the thing off its hinges. She coaxed her eyes to open to slits, but Max's big shoulder blocked her view.

"Tell me I do not smell Whisper in your bed, Max," Alec growled in a voice she scarcely recognized. Maybe it was the drug.

"Get out, Alec," Max said without turning away from Whisper. "You're disturbing us."

He arched his hips, but he wasn't directly over her. A sharp pinch to her side made her cry out. To an enraged man, she imagined it sounded like a moan of ecstasy instead of annoyance that the idiot pinched her. Alec roared and leaped across the room. He grabbed his brother by the hair and jerked him off the bed.

"Don't," she tried yelling, but it came out feeble and small.

Seeing Max in all his naked glory made her turn her head, but she had no idea when he'd removed the rest of his clothing. At some point, she must have zoned out. The comforter still half covered her, but with one thigh out and her sides bare, it was obvious she was naked as well.

Bile rose in her throat at the sound of Alec punching his brother. "You don't touch her! Ever!"

"Stop," she pleaded and managed to roll over. The comforter tangled around her legs and sent her pitching over the side of the bed. She hit the floor in a weakened heap. In seconds, Alec was there and lifted her up into his arms. He crushed her to his chest to the point that she could barely breathe. Well at least she'd gotten him to stop hurting Max.

"Get out," Alec ordered.

Whisper tried getting her face above the cover and off his chest but failed.

"This is my room," Max answered, his voice full of his usual humor, although she thought she detected a funny inflection on his words. Maybe his lip was swollen. For some reason she felt guilty, but this was his fault—his dumb ass plan.

"I mean get out of the apartment," Alec ground out. "I don't want to see you the rest of the day—maybe never."

"Alec." Whisper managed to raise her head. She got her eyes open but was pretty sure she looked drunk as hell.

Alec looked down at her, and the rage in his expression was palpable. "You fucking asshole, you drugged her! You're dead as soon as I help her. Dead, Max!"

This time his brother seemed to get it. Max dressed in a hurry and was out of the room in moments. She heard the front door slam, and

Alec sank down on the bed with her on his lap. He glanced over his shoulder at the rumpled sheets and cringed then stood and carried her out and across the hall to another room. She figured this one was his and didn't protest when he laid her on the bed. She kept waiting for him to yell at her and call her a whore, but his hold turned gentle as he pushed her hair from her hot face.

"Don't worry," he murmured. "I'm going to fix this. He'll die for hurting you."

Even though he was angry, she heard the pain in his voice, too, and vowed as soon as she could come out of her stupor, she'd explain everything to him. Max hadn't done anything to her. The worse she'd suffered was embarrassment and a little pinch. She didn't want Alec thinking his brother had betrayed him or for him to feel like he had an obligation to hurt the family member closest to him. For some reason, she was pretty sure Alec meant to kill his own brother.

Chapter Ten

Whisper woke up feeling refreshed, to her surprise. She had no headache like she expected from the drug. In fact, she felt like she'd gotten some much needed rest as she hadn't been sleeping well the last few days. A look at the clock showed it to be just after ten, and from the darkness outside, she guessed it was still night.

Remembering Alec's promise to hurt his brother, she tossed the covers back and sprang up out of bed. Alec had put her bra and panties back on, and he'd left her to sleep in his bed. She found her clothes folded on a nearby chair and slipped into them. Barefoot, she left his room in search of him. As soon as she walked into the living room, he stood up from the couch and faced her. Worry etched his handsome face.

"Are you okay?" he asked.

She nodded. "I'm fine. I wanted to talk to you about Max."

Alec crossed the room in two long strides to cup her face. "You don't have to worry about him, baby. I'll take care of it. I can only imagine what a woman in this situation feels, and if you need to talk to someone, I mean professionally, I will pay—"

She put fingers over his mouth, and he fell silent. "I wasn't raped."

Confusion clouded his eyes, and then they widened. She knew what conclusion he jumped to, that she'd wanted it.

"No, not that." She almost laughed at the absurdity of the situation. Max had done more harm than good. When this was all over and Alec understood what happened, they still wouldn't be together. "We didn't have sex at all. He was pretending, to get you to go off on him. I guess that worked like a charm. I'm sorry. I didn't want this, but Max definitely didn't hurt me. He never touched me like that."

Alec gripped her arms. "Don't cover for him, Whisper. I know the charm my kind has, and Max has a lot even while he acts like an idiot most of the time. He should be punished for—"

"For loving you?"

He frowned at her.

On impulse, she leaned up and kissed his lips. Longing took hold, but she pushed it aside. With care, she explained everything that happened and everything they said. She even included the nonsense about him and Max being able to shift into leopards, but Alec didn't laugh at that part. In fact, he seemed more annoyed that Max had told her.

Alec released her and walked over to the couch. She felt like he'd abandoned her, but she squashed the feeling.

"I didn't want you to know about that."

She blinked at his back. "Come again?"

He peered over his shoulder at her. "About our ability to shape shift. We don't share the secret with humans."

"Humans." Okay, her mind had gone dull. All this time, she'd thought Alec was the sane one.

He paced. "You've been visited a couple times by the leopard. Tell me what you noticed different about it."

She wanted to tell him to seek help but decided to humor him. With her arms wrapped around her in an effort to comfort her broken heart, she crossed to the couch and sat down. "I know this sounds crazy, but it seemed like there were two of them. I don't know, but maybe it was small differences in the coat or the attitude." *Whisper, why are you even having this conversation? The man and his brother need help.*

"Baby."

She flinched at his use of the endearment but looked up at him. All of a sudden, Alec changed. One minute he was standing there as a man, and the next his clothes were in a pile on the floor, and the leopard was there. Whisper shrieked and drew her feet up. "Impossible, impossible!"

The leopard took a step in her direction, but she held up a hand. "No, don't!"

He stopped moving.

Whisper drove a hand through her hair and closed her eyes. She shook from head to toe. Over and over, she replayed the events from the time she met Alec in the hall and the leopard coming out of his apartment, to the nights it visited her. The only time she was afraid of it was that first night, but not after she got to know the men—its counterparts. *This is insane. I can't believe it. The drug must have addled my wits.*

Alec shifted back and began to dress. "It's real, baby."

"Don't... Please don't call me baby."

He sat down across from her, and she could almost feel his misery, although she didn't know why he should feel that way. What she felt beyond shock, she didn't know.

"I don't know what to say. Whisper, I would never hurt you. Nor—now that I know the truth of what he did—would my brother. We aren't human, but we're still men."

"You're not!" She covered her mouth for a minute, and he stared at her. "I don't know how to take this. I want to go home, *please.*"

"I wouldn't hold you against your will. Of course you can go." He stood up with her when she did. Whisper tried to hide her fear, but she was pretty sure it was coming through loud and clear. On one hand she wanted to be with him more than anything. Then again, she was confused and scared about what he had just showed her. She needed to get away and hope her head would clear.

Alec stepped aside so she could get to the door. She zipped past him and ran into the hall. At her own apartment, she realized she had no idea where her purse was, which held her keys.

Alec leaned past her and unlocked the door. She shivered, but he handed her the keys and her purse. She mouthed her thanks because the words didn't come out, and then she hurried inside. With the locked door between them, she was safer but not calmer. How this mess was going to be resolved, she had no idea.

* * * *

Whisper put down the last page of Alec's book. She'd been avoiding him for two weeks, but during that time, he had dropped off the last quarter of his work outside her door. She felt guilty for how she had been treating him, despite the fact that he'd been with another woman. For all she knew he could still be seeing her. The worst of it was that she and he weren't together, so what he did shouldn't matter. Every day she told herself to move on. Now that she knew what he was, it was even better that they didn't work out. Tell that to her body, and to her heart.

She dreamed of him. She looked for him when she had to leave the apartment. A couple times, she'd spotted him going out and once coming home. He nodded in greeting and gave a little half smile, but he never approached. She knew he was doing that for her sake, because she was afraid. All that time, she hadn't seen Max at all and wondered if he was okay. Alec had told him he didn't know if he ever wanted to see him again, but surely he'd changed that when he learned his brother meant well. She hoped so. They were close. If she could have had a good relationship with her sister or even had a brother, she would not give it up for a lover that might not last. Maybe that was because she didn't know what being in love was or what finding the right one entailed.

The truth was, she wanted to go see him, to talk to him. Now that the fear had eased a little, she didn't want to run away. The confusion was still there, but she suspected talking to him would help.

Taking a deep breath, she gathered all the pages of his book together and slipped them in the envelope he'd sent. Then she walked out to the hall and knocked on his door. To her surprise, it swung inward as if someone had left it open. Horror washed over her, and her stomach clenched when she saw the emptiness of the apartment. Almost everything had been moved out except for a few boxes.

"Oh no," she breathed.

"Whisper."

She whirled, and there he stood behind her. All of the emotions she'd thought had settled rose up again, and her heartbeat kicked up a thousand notches. Goose bumps popped out on her forearms. He looked so damn good, she wanted to jump him right there and eat him up. *Get a grip, Whisper. He doesn't care about you. Besides, he's not human. Remember that most of all...but why?*

"You're moving," she said. *Duh.* "I didn't know."

He nodded. "I finally settled on my house. I thought it was time to go."

She half turned away. "Of course. Um...I have your book. It was awesome. All the way to the end, I was on the edge of my seat, but then I've said that a million times. The ending was satisfying, all the loose ends tied up. You're brilliant."

He grinned, and she couldn't miss the joy her words brought him from the way he beamed. "You've said that once or twice, too."

She laughed. "I guess I did." Not knowing what else to say, she handed him the envelope. "Well, I wish you the best in your writing career and in life." She swung away to go back to her place.

"You owe me."

She stopped. "What?"

He tucked the book under his arm and reached for her hand. She shook from the first brush of his fingers. "Three dates. We had a deal to have five, and you gave me only two."

Her brows went up. "But that was so you could get... I mean I don't want to insinuate that—"

"So you're going to renege?"

She sucked her teeth and folded her arms under her breasts.

"You've got a nerve."

"Yes, I do."

She couldn't help herself. She wanted it so bad, to spend time with him, to talk to him. Why? He'd moved on so quickly, hadn't he? And he was what he was. So many questions flitted through her mind about that and what his life had been like growing up being a shifter. Whisper put a hand up to her head and closed her eyes. She tried dredging the resolve to turn him down and walk away.

"For what it's worth," he said, "I didn't sleep with her. I didn't want her. I just wanted to get you out of my head."

Whisper opened her eyes and stared at him. "You don't owe me an explanation. We weren't a couple."

"Weren't we?" That response surprised her. He stepped closer and pulled her into his embrace. "Whisper, from the first moment I met you, thoughts of you consumed me. I wanted to breathe the air you breathed. I wanted to hear your voice and talk to you. I never told anyone about my writing, but I discussed it with you. It meant everything to me to have you approve, and the fact that you were still willing to read it and give me your opinion even when you were angry—that blew me away. My brother was a fool for what he did, but he was right about one thing."

She dared not ask what that thing was. "Is Max okay? You two aren't still mad, are you? I'd hate to be the cause of your relationship being destroyed."

"We're fine," he assured her. "What I'm more concerned with right now is you."

"Alec." She looked down at their clasped hands. Hers trembled, and she hoped he didn't notice. He squeezed them gently and then shook them to get her attention. She glanced up and was swallowed up in the gentleness she saw in his eyes. No, she wasn't afraid anymore. Just as she sensed the leopards wouldn't hurt her, she knew Alec wouldn't. He was an animal and a man.

"I know you're unsure about what I am. It's a lot to take in, but if you'll give me a chance, I promise to answer every question that you have. We'll talk it out as often as you like. I'm not asking for a commitment. Just a few dates."

Whisper licked her lips. She was tempted beyond measure, and there wasn't a reason she could put together to say no. Well, there were several questions. "Um, isn't us being together sort of like me sleeping with an animal? I mean, are you a leopard that can turn into a man? Or vice versa? I'm sorry. I don't mean to offend you."

He chuckled. "I'm not offended. Let me make you dinner, and I will tell you all."

She rolled her eyes. "One thing is for sure, you don't give up easily. Fine. Dinner. But it doesn't look like you have much left in your apartment, unless we're using mine."

"We'll use yours, and then I'll take you to see my house. I hope you'll like it. I wish we could have chosen it together."

"Whoa, slow down, buddy." She shook her head. "One minute you just want a friend with benefits, and now you want me to help you choose silverware. What an about face." She pretended the thought didn't give her intense pleasure. "Let's take it one day at a time."

"Agreed!"

* * * *

Whisper stood up from the blanket and ran across the sand to splash into the water. She used the move to get some space between them, and Alec must have picked up on it because he didn't follow. They'd done a lot of talking over the last couple of dates. This one was their fifth, and she'd elected to go to the beach and have a picnic there. The day was too cool to swim, but that was the bonus. Not many people were out there, so they had a lot of privacy to talk.

What Alec had shared with her about his background and his

people so far helped her understand him better, but it was still foreign. To think there were species, walking among people, who weren't human. Not human exactly but not fully animal.

"Okay?" he asked coming near but not too close. She had to give him props for not pushing, just letting her take her time to get used to the whole idea.

"Yeah, I'm fine." Her heart skipped beats when she saw him and when he was close. The attraction wasn't going away no matter what she learned about him. "It just boggles my mind. Are you an alien?"

He laughed. That was another thing she loved about him. He was never offended by her questions, never angry or impatient. "I was born and raised on earth, in Scotland. My parents brought us over to Maine when I was sixteen. My grandparents are still in Scotland, but they visit the U.S. upon occasion. Other times we go there. We tend to keep track of our ancestry, so I'm pretty sure we are not aliens. Now did some odd magic happen centuries ago? Maybe. No one knows that for sure."

"I read a lot of shifter books," she admitted. "And in them, the authors describe cracking of bones, regrowing muscle and sinew, shrinking and all that. You don't shift that way."

"No." He moved closer. She put her hand out, and he took it. Together they walked down the beach. "As I mentioned, it seems like magic when we change. In an instant we go from man to beast and back again. There is no pain, no hardship. There never was, even when I did it for the first time as a toddler."

"So you don't have to reach puberty or whatever?"

He looked at her like she was speaking a foreign language.

"Shifter books. Sorry."

"No worries. We come to a realization of what we are, and that might happen at birth or at four or even late teens."

"Interesting."

Alec brought her hand to his lips and kissed it. "Whisper, with all you've learned about me, do you think you can accept me as I am?"

"Accept you?" She chewed her lip. Butterflies fluttered in her stomach.

He stopped walking and drew her into his arms. "I want to be with you, Whisper. I know I ran from the truth of what you mean to me, but I'm not afraid anymore."

That shook her. A man as strong and vibrant as Alec admitting that he was afraid. His words went a long way toward helping her to trust him because he opened himself up to her. She was willing to bet he wouldn't admit it to anyone else, and that made her feel special. Warmth spread throughout her system. Was this real love, the kind where two people were meant to be? She'd always avoided thoughts of soul mates just in case it was something people made up and wasn't real.

Alec lifted her chin and kissed her. She trembled in his arms, wanting nothing more than to stay there forever. If she was thinking like that, she must care about him. A lot. *I love you?*

The three words together in her mind scared the hell out of her. What if he changed his mind later? What if some woman like her whore of an ex-friend came along and seduced him into being with her? The thoughts tormented her mind. Then something else hit her. What if his people had some weird ritual for him to claim her as his mate, something humiliating?

She frowned at him. "I'm not doing anything weird."

Alec's eyebrows rose. "What made you say that?"

"I mean it, Alec." She broke out of his arms and ticked off the points on her fingers. "I'm not having sex with you in front of your whole clan. I'm not dancing naked by a silvery moon. I'm not hunting on all fours like an animal…"

Alec roared in laughter, so much that he sank to the sand on his knees and wiped tears from the corners of his eyes. "You are something. I know at least you'll always entertain me."

Whisper wasn't amused. She stood above him with her hands on her hips. "You think it's funny, but I'm not doing it. I'll drop your ass in a heartbeat."

He reached up and dragged her down to land on his chest as he fell back. "I promise, my love, I will never ask you to do those things. Well...the dancing naked for me might be nice."

She rolled her eyes at him and laughed. "Whatever."

"I love you."

She froze. "What?"

"You heard me." He caught her chin and forced her to look at him. "I love you, Whisper. You're amazing. You keep me reeling, and I didn't think I could feel about a woman like I feel about you. It seems too fast, but I feel like my brother did when he met Sarah." Pink tinged his cheeks, and she knew he was embarrassed. She was careful not to let on that she noticed in case he stopped being so open.

"I...I..." she stuttered.

"You don't have to say it in return."

He caressed her cheek, and when she shifted on top of him, she felt his erection. That didn't scare her. Letting herself admit she loved him did.

"I can accept you," she said in a low tone with her gaze directed to his shirt front.

"And I can wait for more." He sat up and lifted her to her feet. "What I can't wait for is to enjoy that sexy body of yours. Come on. We're going home."

They started back to the blanket. "I'm surprised you didn't suggest we do it out here."

He winked. "Trust me, I have no compunctions about ravaging you right here and now, but you just warned me you won't have sex with me in public or I'll find myself kicked to the curb." He sighed as if she'd broken his heart.

"Dramatic much?" She giggled. "And I said *dropped*. Don't try to talk like that. You sound crazy, and it doesn't fit my image of you."

Okay, she admitted that she was happy. That wasn't so hard.

He caught her in a strong embrace that took her off her feet. When his lips covered hers, he stole her breath and had her head spinning. Whisper invited his tongue into her mouth, and moaned in pleasure when he ran a hand down to her ass and squeezed. They hadn't had sex since that night in her apartment against the door. Alec hadn't pushed, but she'd seen his hard-on several times. He wanted her even after seeing all her extra flesh. In fact, he seemed hungry for more.

When he set her on her feet, she scrambled to get their things cleaned up. The sooner she was back in his arms, the better!

Chapter Eleven

Whisper stood in her room in front of Alec while he sat on the bed. She smiled at him as she began peeling off her clothes. His eyes never left her body, and she thrilled in it. If someone was to tell her a few weeks ago she wouldn't be self-conscious stripping in front of a man, she would have told them not without losing forty pounds! Yet, she was confident that Alec thought she was sexy. The evidence was there in the tented pants, and the way the man almost drooled with anticipation. She turned to the side and unbuttoned her jeans. Alec leaned forward when she scooted them down low on her hips. He was without a doubt an ass man, and he loved her big 'ol booty. This was the first time in her life that she didn't resent how wide it spread or how much it stuck out.

"Maybe I should get under the covers," she suggested, teasing but sounding dead serious.

His lips compressed, not exactly the reaction she'd been going for. "Don't you dare. Come here, Whisper. I want you to understand that it's okay. I'm not going to hurt you, and my brother will never do what he did to you again."

Crap. She'd overdone it. The man didn't realize Max didn't scare her. She was more worried about *him* at this point, but she hadn't had a chance to talk to Alec about him. Something told her Alec was going to be very protective of her. Warmth spread throughout her system with the knowledge. No man had ever thought of her as a delicate treasure to be handled with care. She liked it, but she would put bra-man in his place if need be.

She walked over to him and stood between his legs. Alec drew in a sharp breath and rested his hands on her hips. "Damn it, baby, you drive me insane. I can't believe I went so long without you in my life. I feel... Hell, I don't know how I feel."

She leaned into him, loving how he pressed his mouth to her belly and kissed her there. Desire coiled in her belly and spread outward. "That's the one thing I find to be true in the books," she commented.

"Hm?" He was busy working her jeans farther down her legs and paused with the exposure of her dimpled thighs. She had a small twinge of annoyance at their state, but Alec acted like he was given a gift, so she didn't sweat it.

"Being what you are," she explained. "It makes you love me because I'm your mate."

"No!" His head snapped up, and she jumped. "Don't believe that. Whisper, do you think I would have looked your way if you weren't the most beautiful woman I have ever seen? Do you think I would have continued to pursue you if your personality didn't match? Yes, I was hooked on you quickly, but that's because of *you*, not because of some fate that makes you the one. Never forget, I love you for you, not because my genes drive me to."

"I won't," she murmured. All here worries dissipated, and even if she wasn't used to Alec being a shape-shifter, she knew what she felt was real. She loved him. Without question, she did. "I love you, Alec."

His fingers spasmed on her hips, and he closed his eyes dipping his head. "I won't ask you if you're sure. Just say it again for me, baby. Let me hear the words."

She stroked his hair, luxuriating in the silkiness of his curls. "Alec, I love you. I'm sure of it. I love you with all my heart."

He jumped to his feet and raised her into his arms to carry around to the side of the bed. With tenderness that made her tear up, he laid her on the bed and then followed her down. He made short work of both of their clothing, and they lay side by side naked. Whisper didn't try hiding her oversized, somewhat saggy breasts. Alec feasted on them with his eyes and then his lips. She arched into the touch and moaned when he sucked harder, going from one nipple to the other.

"Alec…"

"Say my name again," he demanded. She did as she was told, and he raised her thigh to push his big, thick cock deep into her already wet pussy. Whisper keened in bliss. Alec ground into her so roughly, so fast, that all she could do was hang onto him and enjoy it. The impact of their bodies crashing together sent her over the edge. She came screaming, but Alec didn't let up for an instant. He pounded into her, rolled her to her back and climbed on top of her. With her legs up over his shoulders, Alec gripped the backs of her thighs and drove home repeatedly. Her orgasm built a second time, but this round was stronger. The sensations came from somewhere deep and were so strong, she couldn't bite down on her cries.

"Too much, too much," she pleaded, but he didn't back off. If anything, her words drove him wilder. The sounds of his invasion into her pussy seemed loud in her ears. The smack of his pelvis to hers and the slap of his balls on her ass had her shaking and weak. "I don't know about this. It's never been this strong," she whimpered.

"This is your g-spot, honey," he explained, "and when you come it will be more powerful than you've ever experienced. Hold on for me, my love. I will please you."

Hold on? He must be crazy. I can't. I just can't… The orgasm slammed through her from her core out to every part of her body. She thought she felt it in her toes, and her head became so light, she couldn't think straight. Where she'd been screaming before, now the words were lost in her inability to form them. For a few seconds, she thought she fainted. Tears wet her face, but she couldn't remember starting to cry. In her ear, Alec murmured his love over and over. His hold tightened, and he arched once more before his come flooded her channel. A shudder passed between them. Whisper wasn't sure if it was hers or his, but it didn't matter. They were one.

Sometime later, she woke in Alec's arms and yawned. She was worn to a frazzle, and her girly parts were sore as hell. She snuggled closer in her lover's embrace. "Alec, are you sleeping?"

"No, baby."

"I was thinking."

"Hm?" His voice was thick, making it sexier than usual. She shivered in desire.

Calm down, girl, you know you can't take this big man again until you heal. Damn, I should be a shifter. "Is there any way I can become like you?"

He raised his head and looked into her eyes. "Where did that come from?"

"I just wondered." Embarrassment made her look away. Alec didn't like that. He always made her look at him if she did that while they were talking. She took a deep breath and continued. "I just wish we could be closer, or that I could satisfy you as much as you need. I know you could have gone on if I wasn't so sore."

"Don't for one second think that you don't satisfy me, baby," he insisted. "You're everything that I need and more." He kissed her, and she nuzzled into his chest. "Aside from that, over time, we become closer. You will not be a shifter exactly, but there are dormant abilities in humans that never get accessed. I have heard of some of these coming alive over time when one of my kind mates with a human."

"Interesting."

"Anyway, don't be afraid. There's no way I am ever letting you go. I will treasure all that you give me as a gift, and wait for you as long as it takes you to heal."

Her breath wavered as she breathed out. "I've never been loved so deeply."

He grinned down at her. "You've not seen anything yet."

She slapped at his chest. "I look forward to it. Now, about Max. I'm worried about him. Should we find him a new mate?"

He shook his head. "I'm afraid there's only ever been one mate for anyone like us. If one or the other passes, the one left spends their life alone. More often than not, they die before old age."

Whisper's heart constricted. "Uh-uhn, I'm not accepting that. Max deserves happiness, and you can be damn sure I'm going to find the right woman for him so he can love again."

Alec chuckled. "I have the feeling my brother is in trouble."

She frowned. "Hey, that's a good thing."

"If you say so." The grin on his face spread.

"Okay, you'll see. I'm going to have that man tiptoeing through the garden of happiness in no time."

Alec groaned and rolled off the bed. "Fine. Come on. If I can't make love to you right now, we can at least eat, and then we will discuss your strategy for punishing my brother—I mean helping his love life."

When Whisper ran after him to punch him for what he started to say, Alec took off out of the bedroom and down the hall. She was in hot pursuit, knowing that this time he wouldn't go far, and no one would steal him away.

The End

Shira

Chapter One

Shira huddled beneath the overhang to the side of the door. She couldn't imagine anyone would be coming or going in this downpour, but she'd rung every bell, and no one answered. The longer she stood in the rain, the more soaked she got. At least with the narrow ledge overhead, she could lessen the pelts to her face.

A chill raced down her spine, and she shifted her shoulders. Already, she could feel the ache in her muscles. Tomorrow, she would be stiff and sore. Yet, that was better than pain in the usual way she got it.

A sound to her right caught her attention, and she perked up. Someone was coming out. She straightened her shoulders and reached into her pocket for her keys. After tugging the useless hat lower on her head, she jangled the keys in her hand as she approached the door. A man stepped out.

"Really coming down, isn't it?" she muttered and zipped past him into the dry hall. The man might have said something in response, but she didn't wait around to hear. She only hoped her little act worked, as if she was a tenant just getting home and glad she didn't have to use her keys to get into the building.

Before she'd run away, she never would have had the guts to pull that stunt. Maybe her life was taking a turn for the better with the decision to leave Sam. Virginia was home, and he'd acted like he was doing her a favor moving back here after five years in Maryland. In reality, he was just running after a bigger, better position in Emergency Room medicine. The hospital where he worked now had stroked his ego, like everyone did, including her own mother, and Sam had made the decision to come. He hadn't even told her until a week before they needed to have everything packed and move down to his new house.

Shira took the elevator. While she had rung every bell to be let into the building, there was still the hope that Whisper was just asleep and hadn't heard the buzzer. Of course she could be out for the night. If that was the case, Shira would wait at her door.

The elevator dinged, and the doors slid open. She stepped out and walked down the hall. As she approached a turn in the passage, she checked the numbers on each apartment's entrance. Her stomach muscles tightened. What if Whisper didn't want to help? No, she couldn't think like that. Everything would be fine, and she would have a warm bed to sleep in tonight. Whisper would understand.

Then again, will she remember me?

She peered down at her figure. Slimmer than she was in high school, she didn't think she'd changed that much over the years. Thirty-four wasn't so far away from eighteen. Thinking that, she almost laughed, but wasn't in the mood.

At Whisper's door, she pressed the bell and waited. The chimes echoed in the apartment beyond, so she knew it was working. When no one answered, she pressed the bell again. The hope she'd bolstered herself with was fading fast. Maybe she shouldn't have come. To go begging for help from a woman who hadn't exactly been a friend in school was lame. Whisper might think she was crazy, or a bum.

She twisted her cold fingers together in front of her and hesitated another few seconds. No, this was a bad move. She swung away from the door just as the locks were being undone. New hope rose in her, and she turned back.

The door opened to the handsome, if scruffy, face of a man. His blond hair, in need of a cut, hung all about his head, and he looked like he hadn't shaved in days. What she could see of his clothes was rumpled as if he'd slept in them. Despite that, he gave off a sexy, dangerous air. His broad shoulders and big chest, paired with the size of the hand curved around the door made her take a step back.

"What," he snapped.

"I think I might..." she began. This could be Whisper's boyfriend or husband. She hesitated. "Is Whisper home?"

His eyebrows shifted higher. "*You* know her?"

Was she too low class to know Whisper? Maybe he hadn't put the emphasis on the word *you* like she thought. His presence scrambled her senses, and she was tired, so she couldn't be sure.

"Yes, we went to school together. I thought I would look her up," Shira explained. She tried to sound cheerful like this was a friendly visit but was sure she'd failed. "Is she in?"

"No."

He gave no explanation other than that, and Shira waited.

The man sighed. He swung the door wider and stood up straighter. For some reason, he must have been almost bent in half, because when he did, he towered almost a foot above her. Shira didn't mean to allow the squeak of fear to escape. The man was unnecessarily big. She took another step in retreat.

"She's out of town with her boyfriend visiting family," he told her. "I don't expect them back for a while."

"Oh."

All her hopes came crashing down. There was nothing else to say. Whisper had been her last resort. She didn't have an extensive family to go to. There was only her mother and an uncle she would never risk asking for help.

"Thank you." She turned and walked down the hall. In the lobby, she stopped at the door, and the tears gathered. She would have to go back.

The skies had no mercy as she moved out into the storm. Water dripped down her back, freezing her to her core. Her shoes sloshed on her feet, and she huddled behind the thin jacket. While it was midsummer, the evening had turned chilly. The trek here had taken the last of her money, so she would have to walk to Sam's house. Not that it would matter since she was already late.

Hours later, her feet hurt, and her thighs burned. She sneezed incessantly and couldn't stop shivering. On the side of a busy street, she tried extra hard to keep from being run down. Dizziness and exhaustion made that difficult. A car drew up beside her, and Shira's blood ran as cold as her body seeing it.

The passenger side door swung open, and the sharp command, "Get in," rang out from within. Shira didn't dare disobey. She climbed into Sam's car and buckled the seatbelt. He drove in silence, his hands gripping the steering wheel as if it was the only thing keeping him from strangling her. She didn't think that was the reason because as far as she knew nothing had ever kept him from hitting her.

Every now and then, she peered at him out of the corner of her eye. He was handsome in his way, clean-shaven, hair perfectly ordered. He wore an expensive suit that had not one wrinkle. Despite all of that, he didn't look as good as the man she'd met earlier at Whisper's apartment.

That's probably because I hate him.

"Weren't we supposed to have dinner tonight to celebrate my new position and the new house?" Sam asked.

"Yes." She had learned long ago to keep her words simple and to the point.

"Yet, you're not dressed."

He eyed the jeans she'd worn and the old sneakers. She had dressed for comfort for the trip to Whisper's place. Three weeks ago, she had looked Whisper up to find out where she lived and had plotted the bus route.

"I'm sorry." Her voice trembled, and she bit down to try to gain control. In a minute, he would notice the bag on her lap. Who was she kidding? He never would have been out here on this road if he didn't know she had run away. The fact that she'd made him late for his reservation was bad enough. Sam didn't like his plans to be interfered with.

"Oh we'll go to the restaurant. I'm hungry. Maybe you've eaten wherever you were."

She opened her mouth to protest, but clamped it shut before uttering a word. Her stomach growled. She hadn't had a bite since morning. Nerves had taken her appetite.

A short while later, they pulled into the restaurant's parking lot. Sam reached across to nab her bag from her cold fingers. She didn't try to hold on, and he tossed it in the back seat of his jag. Sam got out of the car and came around to open her door. She gritted her teeth against sore muscles and followed him to the entrance.

They were seated quicker than Shira had expected, but then she shouldn't have questioned Sam's willingness to cover anyone's palm with money as long as he got what he wanted.

She sat across from him in silence and picked up the menu the waiter had offered to her. When the man returned, Shira was about to tell him her order when Sam cut her off.

"She's not that hungry tonight. Why don't you bring me the prime rib with two helpings of mixed vegetables on the side."

"Of course, sir. Anything to drink before that?"

"If you could bring a bottle of your best chardonnay, that would be great," he ordered. Shira sat stark still. Her stomach again made its protest, but she didn't say a word. Anger and humiliation vied for dominance inside her. He knew she was hungry, but he punished her. What could she say anyway? She had no money of her own. He'd made sure of that, pushing her to quit her job six months ago and threatening to get her fired if she didn't. Sam wanted her dependent on him, and he had succeeded in getting her to that place. She was beginning to think she would never get free of him.

Sam sat in front of her, discussing his job and prospects between bites. Shira kept a pleasant expression on her face the entire time, hands clutched in her lap. She knew when they got back to his house, she would be in trouble. He was always civil when they were out, even funny and entertaining sometimes. Yet, when they were alone and she'd pissed him off, that's when the hammer would fall. He smiled at her and winked at a joke he'd made. His teeth were even and white. She knew they got that way by his meticulous care and time in the mirror. The man took way longer than her in the bathroom each morning or whatever shift he had to work at the hospital. Up until now, the only consolation Shira was able to enjoy was that he'd often take double shifts. That allowed her to heal until the next punishment.

How had she ended up in this position? She'd been a strong woman with prospects of her own. She'd intended to go to school and major in child development. Her dream was to own a daycare center, but stuck with Sam it would never happen. Her world had to revolve around him. He'd said so the day he insisted she move in with him. By then, it was too late for her. Sam had his claws in her emotionally and physically.

"Where did you intend to go?" he asked without warning.

She jumped and twisted her hands together in her lap. "I don't know. I didn't have a plan."

"To your mother?" He chuckled. "She loves me. I suspect more than she loves you. I can do no wrong in her opinion." He waved his glass of wine, amusement lighting his cruel gaze. "Might have to do with the fact that I pay her rent and bought her the car she and her deadbeat boyfriend drive. What lengths would she go to if I actually bought her a house outright?"

Shira dug her nails into her pants legs. "I wouldn't know. Maybe you should ask her."

He narrowed his eyes, nostrils flaring. "Careful, Shira, you don't want to piss me off worse than you already have with your stunt tonight."

A sob rose in her throat, but she forced it down. "I think it can't get any worse."

He dragged his napkin across his mouth and tossed it aside. Then he pushed his chair back, raising a hand to signal the waiter. "Let's find out, shall we? Time to go."

With a sense of doom, Shira watched him settle the check and come around to help her from her chair as if she was someone precious to him. He laid her hand on his arm with deceptive gentleness, and they headed out to the street.

Chapter Two

At the first light, with the rain coming down in sheets, he pulled the car to a stop and drove his hand into her mouth. Shira's head snapped back, and she cried out. He almost never hit her in the car. That meant she had pushed him beyond his limit.

Tears drenched her face, and the metallic taste of blood filled her mouth. She pressed against the car door, feeling in the darkness for the door handle. Sam took off before she could find it and tooled the vehicle too fast for her to risk jumping out. She prayed he would slow down. Otherwise, they risked hydroplaning. He didn't care. He shook his hand and growled in annoyance.

"You made me hurt myself," he complained. "These are my money-makers, and a lowly bitch like you can't be allowed to risk them."

"I'm sorry."

"Oh, you better be." He grinned, staring at the road ahead. "No, you're *going* to be."

Panic set in. She directed her gaze from one side of the road to the other. She didn't look forward to going back out in that mess, but she had no choice. She didn't think she could stand it one more time, the cruelty, the beatings. Tears flooded her eyes, and she sniffed. Long ago, she'd learned to hide how terrified he made her, because that gave him satisfaction. Tonight, she had no control. Sobs rose no matter how hard she tried to quell them, and Sam laughed.

They were on a quiet back road. She had no idea how close they were to his house as it was too dark, and she wasn't familiar with this area. Now was her chance—do or die. She flipped the lock and threw the door open. The ground came up hard and fast when she unbelted herself and jumped out. The fact that the side of the road was mud and grass helped break her fall, but the impact still hurt.

Behind her, tires squealed. *Get up and run, Shira. Come on. Do it!*

She staggered to her feet and started off in the opposite direction from him, but her movements were sluggish at best. He grabbed her arm, and she swung at him. He backhanded her, and she landed in the mud once again. Shira cried out. Above her, Sam raised his fist. She stared at him in terror. He looked like a demon with his dark hair plastered to his forehead and water running off his angry face.

"Please," she begged.

He raised his arm higher. The growl seemed to come from all sides, and the cat that followed from nowhere. The beast was huge, and Shira thought it might be a leopard. If it was, it was the biggest one she'd ever seen. The thing was all muscle, highlighted by the flashing lightning and rain slicking off its smooth physique. She scrambled backward on her hands and feet, but the cat wasn't coming at her. Sam screamed at a high pitch she'd never heard before when the leopard leaped at him. He hit the ground, letting out a cry of pain. She watched unable to move when he flipped over and scrambled back to his car. The cat gave chase, but Sam was able to jump into his jag and slam the door. Shira couldn't believe he actually threw the car in reverse, did a one eighty, and sped off down the dark road. He'd left her there.

The rain continued to come down with lightning flashing at intervals. Shira sat stark still, peering into the darkness. She had no idea where the leopard went, but she couldn't see or hear it. After some time, her fear eased, and she struggled to her feet. She swayed but managed to stay up.

Were you a figment of my imagination? You saved me either way, and Sam believed you were real.

Sam had taken her bag with him and her ID, but it didn't matter. He was gone. *I'm free.* She took a step in the direction he hadn't been heading when he left. As if on cue, the rain let up and then stopped. No matter how bad she ached or how far she had come already, she wouldn't die out here. A better life was coming somehow. She was determined to make it true.

Not twenty minutes later, a car came along the road. Her heart hammered in her chest, and she stopped. Whoever it was, was moving fast. Shira whimpered. She took a step toward the ditch. Goodness if she fell down there, she wasn't climbing out.

The car slowed and rolled to a stop. She had to be thankful at least it wasn't Sam. When the man stepped out, she didn't know if she should be relieved or scared all over again. "It's you," she said.

The light from the interior of the car illuminated his face. He was breathing hard as if he'd been running. She frowned at him.

"Max," he said. "My name is Max. Would you like a ride?"

"I…" All of a sudden the weariness of what she'd been through came over her, and she couldn't have said no if she wanted to. She nodded, and he guided her to the passenger side. Shira dropped into the seat. Her arms wouldn't obey her to buckle herself in, so when Max got in on the other side, he reached across to do it for her. "Th-Thank you."

He grunted in response and started the car. They were off down the road, but Shira saw no more than that. Exhaustion would not be denied any longer, and she fell into a deep sleep.

* * * *

Max propped his feet up on the railing and leaned back in his chair. He pondered the day. The rain had stopped, and the air was clean and fresh. That only served to annoy him. The day didn't need to be this nice, especially with his mood.

He caught the sound of her movement as soon as she woke. Her scent had been disturbing the entire night before. She smelled sweet like candy, and she stirred his hunger—but not for food. That pissed him off, too, so he decided to keep his distance from her. She could get going now that the storm was over and she'd gotten some rest. He didn't know why he'd brought her here of all places anyway.

"You were the man at Whisper's apartment," she said from the doorway behind him. Max didn't turn around.

"So? I was checking on her things like she asked me to."

"It was such a big coincidence that I ran into you on the road." Now she was making conversation. Why couldn't she just go? He closed his eyes, because what he really wanted to do was turn around and stare at her.

There was no coincidence of their meeting the second time. He'd seen the devastation in her eyes when he told her about Whisper being out of town. That expression had hounded him until he tracked her. Not a big deal for his kind, even in the rain.

Rather than answer, he shrugged.

"I-I could cook you breakfast," she offered.

He glared at her over his shoulder. "In other words, you're hungry, and you want me to feed you." He didn't know where his light-heartedness had gone. The entire time his brother dated Whisper, he'd joked around, even if he was fighting despair and depression. Now, he couldn't muster a smile to save his life. Maybe it had to do with the parade of stupid women Whisper had marched by him, trying to tempt him into falling in love again. She couldn't know being human that he mated once and that was it.

She frowned. "Is this attitude a morning thing, or are you always an ass?" After the words left her mouth, she slapped a hand over her lips. When she winced, Max's anger flared again.

"*He* do that to you?"

She dipped her head and redirected her gaze anywhere but at his face. "No. Um, I should go."

"Three eggs, bacon, and sausage. I like them fried hard, and don't be skimpy with the meat. Also toast and coffee!"

She spun away and marched back into the house. Max let his gaze drop to her ass. Despite how slender she was, there was a roundness there that he found sexy. His cock twitched in his pants, but he forced himself around in his chair and closed his eyes. A woman like that didn't need someone like him for a bed partner. He would have to be blind not to recognize the signs of abuse—and anything but a leopard shifter not to smell her fear.

When she called him in to eat, Max walked into the kitchen to the scent of food and coffee. He breathed deep and noticed the full plate waiting. She'd taken his charge seriously not to skimp on the meat. Four slices of bacon and three sausages sat on his plate with more in the center of the table. He hid his approval from his expression and took a seat across from her.

"What's your name?" he asked.

"Shira."

Pretty. "That's unusual."

"I was named after my great-grandmother on my father's side. I don't know where she got the name, but I've always liked the uniqueness of it." She offered a slight smile, and Max blinked against the sunshine in it. Irritation rolled along his spine. He focused on her plate rather than her face. She'd given herself one egg and one slice of bacon with a half a piece of toast. He grabbed the tongs and piled more meat on her plate. She squeaked in protest like a little mouse.

"You're too thin."

"Sorry."

He thought he'd insulted her and searched his mind for a compliment he didn't mind giving, but none he could think of wouldn't give her the impression he was interested. He most certainly was *not*.

"You have a beautiful house," she said, distracting him from his thoughts. "I can see where this place was once amazing and where it can be again."

Max muttered his thanks. "I didn't put much effort into choosing it. My brother moved and threw all of my stuff out."

Shira blinked at him, eyes wide. The cute wrinkle in her nose told him she thought he was poor and a bum. He decided not to enlighten her to the fact that he and his brother had amassed a small fortune in real estate, and he bought this house with cash. Let her think what she wanted. None of it mattered anyway since he'd lost Sarah. Not the money, not his life.

Shira licked bacon oil from her lip, and he found himself staring. His cock was so hard it was painful, and he shifted in his chair. Her hair was cut to her shoulders and straight, and it framed her soft features. Slender, she had small breasts, that scarcely caused a rise in her blouse and yet, he'd never seen a more beautiful African American woman. The large chocolate eyes were so full of innocence and pain, he almost winced from their affect on him. She couldn't know how vulnerable she appeared, he thought, which was why he couldn't have anything to do with her.

Not that he was looking for a lover. Since Sarah died, there had been no one. Despite the fact that a leopard shifter experienced a more aggressive sex drive, and he was no exception, he allowed his desires to go unsatisfied since her death. He would rather suffer than find solace in another woman's arms, least of all this tiny human.

"Do you know if there's any place hiring nearby?"

He looked up from his plate. "What are your qualifications?"

She hesitated. "Well I used to work in child care, at a center. Not a long time, so I don't have that much experience. The place I worked at was managed by a friend, and she did me a favor. I don't expect any other facility to hire me without a reference."

He was about to ask her wouldn't the friend give her a glowing reference even if it wasn't true, but she beat him to the punch.

"My friend and I had a falling out," she explained. "But I'll take anything. I need the money."

"You can be my housekeeper and cook," he blurted and then kicked himself for the impulse. He was a fool.

Her mouth dropped open. "Are you serious?"

He frowned. "If you're too good for that…"

"No! I'll do it." Her smile blinded him once again, and Max gritted his teeth. "I guess you need someone to get this place in shape. I mean have you ever cleaned it?"

"Does your mouth always run away with you?" he growled.

She jumped and shrank back as if she expected him to hit her. "I'm sorry. I never learn. You'd think I'd know how to shut it by now. I'm too blunt. I'm so sorry."

"Relax." He rose from his chair and took his dishes to the sink. Keeping his back to her, he drew in breath after deep breath, trying to calm down. On one hand he wanted to draw this woman he didn't know into his arms and ease her fears. On the other, he longed to beat the man to a bloody pulp who had made her feel like she had to apologize for everything she said. "You have clothes?"

"Um." She hesitated. "I lost my bag, but I can pick up some more things later."

He ignored the explanation. "You can wear another one of my T-shirts."

"Another one?" she squeaked.

He peered at her. The silly woman had just realized he'd changed her clothes the night before. He couldn't put her to bed wet. "I didn't look."

Her brows lowered like she didn't believe him, but she didn't pursue that line of conversation. "Thank you. I'll wash my clothes out and then clean yours when mine are dry."

"Whatever." Max had to get out of there before he did something he would regret. He left her in the kitchen doing dishes and walked outside to get into his car. Something told him he made a big mistake offering her a job, but he couldn't take it back now. The engine roared to life, and he peeled out of the driveway, putting as much space as possible between himself and Shira.

Chapter Three

Max. Shira chided herself for repeating his name. She was attracted to her new boss. She could admit that. The man was sexy as hell and so tall. After what she'd been through, she had no business thinking about another man, but she couldn't help it. Max was like a big teddy bear. She didn't know why she felt like that, but he didn't scare her. Not too much. She smiled to herself as she dried and put up the dishes. He was gruff and rude, and she'd ended up sassing him. His roughness around the edges didn't offend her. Shira had been hurt, so she knew another person in pain when she saw one. Max was like a wounded animal, and when a beast is injured, they tended to strike out at whoever was nearest. That meant her. Still, he hadn't scared her off.

Staying in the area wasn't ideal, of course. If she wanted to start a new life, she needed to get as far away from Sam as possible. That would take money. She would stay with Max long enough to make bus fare and some extra to live off of until she found a job in whatever city she chose. The housekeeper gig would be good, too, because it meant she could hide out in Max's house most of the time. There was less chance of her running into Sam. The night before, she'd fallen into a deep sleep when she got into Max's car, so she had no idea how far he drove from where he picked her up. She didn't imagine it was the next state over. That would be too good to be true.

She pushed the curtain back at the kitchen window and peered out. There was nothing to see except beautiful trees. From what she'd seen from his front porch, he didn't have close neighbors. That meant when she had to do grocery shopping, Max would have to take her. He could protect her for that time, even if neither of them preferred it.

After she was done straightening up the kitchen, she wandered around the house. Max's place had four bedrooms, and none of them were supplied with even a stick of furnishing, except the master bedroom. She stood in the doorway of that room staring in. *He put me in his bed last night.*

Nervousness tightened the muscles in her stomach, but she was pretty sure he'd slept elsewhere the night before. Where, she didn't know because he didn't even own a couch. The kitchen set was no more than a table and two chairs. They had looked like they were meant as patio furniture rather than a kitchen, but she wasn't one to judge. Could he even afford to hire her?

Shira sighed. They hadn't discussed salary. Max was a big man and a stranger. For all she knew, she could have fallen out of one bad situation and landed into another. Yet, she had no choice. She had to hope that Max was the decent person he seemed to be.

Thinking to dust in his room since there was nowhere else to clean other than sweeping and mopping the floors, she found a rag and some furniture polish under the kitchen sink and headed back into his room. The bedroom set was deep mahogany, heavy wood, and appeared to be brand new. Maybe he'd sunk the last of his money into it. She hoped the landlord wasn't charging him through the nose for rent. Or had he said he owned this place? She doubted it.

When she shifted items on the dresser to wipe it down, she found a picture in a frame turned toward the wall. Shira examined it out of curiosity. The blonde staring back at her in the frame was incredibly beautiful with blue eyes and big, natural-looking breasts. "So this is his type," she mused.

Then it occurred to her that this woman could be the reason he looked so sad. The fact that he'd turned the picture away said volumes. He had a broken heart. She'd maybe left him for another man. *Of course she's out of her mind, and must not have looked at Max. The man is gorgeous! Her loss.*

Shira

In light of finding the photograph, Shira considered Max again. His meanness seemed more turned inward than to her, as if he wanted to punish himself for something. Maybe he'd driven the blonde away. Max was no doubt regretting it big time. She wondered what it was like to be loved that deeply, or for that matter to love someone else to that extent.

She ran her hand over the T-shirt he'd put on her. The shirt was gigantic and hung over one shoulder. All morning, she'd been pulling it up so she wouldn't flash him with one of her small boobs. *Not like he'd be tempted when he liked them busty.* She had never minded her tiny size until she started seeing Sam. Then she was hearing all the time how pathetic her breasts were, how she should get a boob job so she wouldn't be such an embarrassment to him. Sam had never offered to pay for it, and she couldn't afford it on her own. She suspected he thought if she did get implants, people would assume he had pushed her to it. Everything had been about image to him. Sam had a terrible cruelness, and no matter how rude Max was, she didn't believe he was like her ex.

Later that morning, the bell rang when Shira had just finished mopping one of the spare bedroom's floors. She figured she could borrow some blankets and a pillow and sleep down there, because it was for sure she wasn't sleeping in Max's bed again. She dropped the mop and bucket off in the kitchen and headed toward the front of the house. Her stomach knotted, and she twisted her fingers. There was no way Sam would know she was here.

She peeked through one of the windows at the side of the door and spotted a man who looked like delivery personnel. Behind him was a huge truck with a picture of a living room set designed on the side. *How the heck did they find their way out here?*

She opened the door. "Yes?"

"Miss...uh..." He checked his notes. "Miss Shira?"

She almost laughed because Max didn't know her last name. For that matter, she didn't know his either. "Yes."

"We have a delivery for Max Macgregor—a bedroom set, dining room, and living room set."

"Wow, really?" Her eyes widened. Had he gotten it all on credit? Maybe he wasn't as poor as she had assumed. "Can I see your order form, please?"

The guy smiled. "Of course."

After she'd confirmed everything, she let them in, and the man and his partner set up all the furniture. She directed them to the bedroom she'd chosen for her own and hoped Max wouldn't mind. Hers was across the hall and down a little, the farthest from his. She also hoped he wouldn't notice that fact.

After the deliverymen were gone, Shira straightened out her room, shoving furniture into positions she liked better. Max might change it all, but for now she arranged it her way. She didn't know why she felt a slight excitement but put it down to this being one small part of her new life. Sam had stolen five years, and now she was free.

When she was done with her room, she puttered some more about the house. Max didn't show up until late evening, and by then, she had dinner waiting for him.

He came in the side door tracking mud, and she opened her mouth to protest but clamped it shut. He glanced up at her and must have read her displeasure because he said, "What?"

"Nothing. The people delivered the furniture." Her words came out in a rush, and she looped her fingers together. "I hope you don't mind I chose the bedroom at the end of the hall, near the back of the house. If you want, you can move everything. After all it is your house, and I'm just an employee."

"Stop."

She fell silent. Her breaths came in heavy pants, and he walked toward her. She tried holding her ground and then took a step back. Max towered above her and grasped her arms. Electric currents pinged all over her body, and she could do nothing but gape at him.

"You're upset."

"I'm not," she protested.

He frowned. "You talk fast when you're upset."

She pressed her lips together. He tugged her fingers apart.

"You also wring your hands."

"I—"

He looked over her head and scanned the kitchen. Shira could have fallen over when he sniffed the air. "Was someone else here other than the delivery men?"

She broke from his touch and backed up. "Of course not! If you must know, I take exception to you tracking mud in my kitchen."

His blond brow rose, and she chewed on her bottom lip, but then raised her chin. The man had no manners, and if she was going to work for him, he better get some.

"I scrubbed this house top to bottom, and the least you could do is take off your shoes!"

She must be crazy. He was going to fire her before she even got a dime. Max didn't say a word for a long time. He just looked at her. Why oh why did she have to act like this? She never would have gone off that much with Sam. Not without getting her teeth knocked down her throat.

"I'm so—"

"Don't you say it," he growled. He pivoted on his heel and marched over to the door. Shira stood there in amazement while he stripped his shoes off, put them to the side, and then began mopping up his mess. When he was done, he picked up some bags he'd brought in, walked over to her, and shoved them into her arms. "What's for dinner?"

Shira couldn't help feeling like they were an old married couple, but as soon as she had that thought, she pushed it away. There was no sense getting attached to Max. She was going to move on as soon as possible. Besides, why would he want someone like her? "What's this?"

"I'm hungry," he said instead of answering her question.

She rolled her eyes and laughed a little. As she tucked the bags away in her room, she considered the fact that she hadn't laughed in forever. Come to think of it, in the short time she'd known him, Max hadn't smiled once. She wondered what she could do to give him that pleasure.

She left her room and found Max in the dining room, sitting at the head of the table. "I changed my mind."

She put a hand on her hip. "I guess reading minds is included in my job description?"

A twitch at the corner of his mouth got her excited, but she tamped it down.

"Check the bags," he told her. "I can wait until you change. Maybe the blue one?"

She frowned at him, and then it hit her. He'd bought her clothes. A tremor started somewhere deep in her belly. He was a good man. Shira wouldn't let herself care. She couldn't afford to. "Thanks. You didn't have to do that."

He made no response.

"I'll hurry up." She whirled to run back to her room. Searching through the bags, she found several sundresses, a couple pairs of shorts, and some capris. She found assorted tops in various colors and styles. All of the clothes were in her size. The man had a good eye. She couldn't believe it. He'd gone all out, and it wasn't necessary. Tears filled her eyes. Sam had never done anything like that. He'd once shoved money into her hand when they were planning to go to a party and said, "Don't buy anything that would embarrass me." Sometimes she had wondered how he could date a black woman if he was so hung up on how people viewed him, but she learned his sleeping with her was what he considered his one vice. He had a thing for black women that his sense of the perfect image couldn't erase. She'd resented him for that view.

Shira stripped her clothes off and threw on the robe Max had included with the clothes. She ran for the bathroom and took a hasty shower. After she was done, she put on the blue dress he had indicated. Blue wasn't her favorite color. Lilac was, but the dress was pretty, and she wanted to give back to Max in this small way for what he'd done.

As she left her room, she considered whether Max wasn't similar to Sam. Max was still dominant. The fact that he'd found it necessary to tell her which dress he would like to see told her a lot. She wondered what he would say and how he would act if she'd put on the butter yellow dress. Too late now, she didn't go back to change. The man must be starving since it was well after seven.

Tonight she had made lasagna with double the usual amount of meat she put in. She dished two plates up and prepared to warm the food a bit more in the microwave when the phone rang. Shira set the plates down and answered the extension hanging on the kitchen wall. "Hello?"

"Hello?" a man said. The timbre of his voice was deep and sexy, very similar to Max's. In fact if she didn't know he sat waiting in the dining room, she would have thought it was him on the phone.

"Is this Max's brother?" she asked.

Instead of answering, she heard the man speaking to someone in the background. "Baby, there's a woman at Max's house."

"What the hell?" a woman responded. "A woman? Who is it?"

Shira tapped her foot waiting for the exclamations and shock to settle. Apparently, Max didn't entertain much.

"Give me the phone," the woman said, and she came on the line. "Hello? Who is this?"

Shira had been thinking the woman sounded familiar. Now she realized who it was. "Whisper, is that you? This is Shira—from school. You probably don't remember me."

"Shira!" The excitement in Whisper's tone warmed her. "Hey, girl. I can't believe you're at Max's? How did you two meet, and how did you convince his grumpy ass to let you come over?"

Shira suppressed a laugh, but then she sobered and told her old schoolmate how she'd met Max. She left out the part about needing to escape from Sam. That wasn't the kind of thing she wanted to share over the phone, and Max might be listening. For some reason, she didn't want him to know how stupid she was to let a man hurt her for so long. She hadn't intended it to go on, and she couldn't explain how she had lost herself in the process. The one thing she knew was that when the fear set in, that was it. He'd had control.

"Oh, sweetie, I'm sorry I'm not there to see you," Whisper said. She sounded happy with her life, and Shira was jealous, but she was glad Whisper had found someone special and was living. "Can I ask you a favor, though?"

Shira raised her brows. What favor could she do for Whisper? She had nothing. "Um, if I can, sure."

"I'm going to be out here in Maine with my boyfriend's family. He's Max's brother by the way. We'll be here for at least another month. Can you look after Max while I'm gone? He's had a tough time, and I feel like if he let you in, you must be something special. You might be the one to make him realize his life isn't over. Can you do that for me?"

Alarm rose in Shira. She hadn't planned to stay, and looking out for Max wasn't in the program. What could she offer a man like him? He had a broken heart. She couldn't fix a thing, and she was most definitely not special. "I…"

"I'm sorry. I shouldn't put that kind of pressure on you," Whisper said. "Just please think about it, and if it progresses, great. If not, it wasn't meant to be."

"Progresses? Meant to be?" Looking out for him had nothing to do with being meant for him. Shira's hands shook. She hated the hope that sprung up inside of her that a miracle would happen and she'd be able to stick around rather than leave. That was unrealistic. If she was going to learn to be strong again, she had to keep her head out of the clouds. She took in a deep breath and steeled herself. "I will try to cheer him up while I'm here. That's all I can do."

"Thanks, girl."

Shira hesitated and then lowered her voice. "Can I ask you something?"

"Sure."

"Is he okay to work for? I mean, he seems…I don't know. I've had some bad experiences in the past with men, and I don't want to trust my judge of character."

Whisper was quiet for a moment. "He's a great guy. You don't have to worry about Max. He'll take care of you. He might seem rough around the edges and like he has no ambition." She laughed at this. "But he really is brilliant. He has a, um, let's say a wild side, but deep down, he's a pussy cat. He'll never hurt you."

"Is he suicidal?"

"Oh, nothing like that," Whisper assured her. "Their kind has too much pride."

Shira pondered what *their kind* meant, but didn't ask. Whisper's words encouraged her somewhat. "Okay, thanks. Well I should let you speak to him. Hold on."

Shira called Max into the kitchen for the phone and went to heating their food. She didn't mean to listen to the phone conversation, but she couldn't help it.

"Any particular reason you didn't call my cell?" he asked. Shira rolled her eyes. So his rudeness wasn't reserved for strangers. "Oh, yeah, no one called me, so I guess I forgot to charge it."

Shira smothered a laugh. She could imagine Whisper putting him in his place, but she'd also heard the affection in her friend's voice. Whisper obviously loved him like a brother. She wondered how Max felt about Whisper. For some reason a little jealousy rose. Whisper had been plumper with bigger boobs and a good size butt in school. Guys had always been exclaiming over it. Whisper would be the kind of woman he went for.

Stop it, Shira! Damn it, it doesn't matter what he goes for. You're leaving. The best you can do is try to cheer him up like Whisper asked. That's all. So suck it up!

She finished heating their lasagna and went to set the plates on the table. With it, she'd made garlic bread and a pitcher of sweet tea. When all was in readiness, she sat down at the table to wait for Max.

At last, he walked into the dining room to take his seat. She'd piled his plate high with food but would heat him more if he wanted it. "I hope you like it," she said. The one thing Shira could be confident about was that she was a decent cook. Not spectacular, but no one would go hungry because of her.

He eyed her plate. She'd made sure to put a decent amount on it so he wouldn't complain, and he nodded. "Tastes good. Thanks."

The compliment was unexpected if plain in its delivery. She appreciated it all the more. Max wasn't just flattering her. "I'm glad you like it." She considered making conversation. One thing that seemed to help people who were feeling down was talking about what was bugging them. Not that she planned on exploring her own feelings. "So, I was cleaning up in your room, and I came across a picture."

Okay, great way to start a conversation, Shira. You're an idiot.

Max grunted.

"The woman in the picture is beautiful. Was she your wife?"

He gave her a hard look, which seemed to say drop it.

"I know how hard it is when the relationship with the person you love so much doesn't work out. It can be tough to walk away and let them go." She drifted off feeling lame. Was he even listening? Max sat there tucking into the food with gusto. He put away the huge slice of garlic bread in a couple bites and drained half his glass of tea at a shot.

When he set the glass down, he eyed her. "Let's get this straight just to settle your curious mind," he began. Shira shifted in her chair. "Sarah was my mate, soon to be my wife. She did not leave me. She died."

And the conversation went to hell. Shira couldn't make herself respond. She hadn't made him feel better. She had dredged up painful memories and come off to Max as if she was just being nosy.

"Oh." Rather than say I'm sorry, which she was, she kept quiet. Saying that had pissed him off before, and if she hadn't set him off just now, she wanted to avoid it. As she pushed her food around on her plate, the nature of her job occurred to her. Did housekeepers sit down to dinner with their employers? Probably not. Embarrassment took her appetite. She jumped to her feet. "I should wash the pots."

"Sit down, Shira. You're not done."

Her hands fluttered above her dish, and she curled her fingers into her palms to keep them still. "I shouldn't be in here eating with you. I know housekeepers don't do that."

"We're not keeping to tradition."

Damn, did he have to be so deadpan about everything? Irritation rose in her. "Are you going to spend the rest of your life feeling sorry for yourself? Or are you going to live, because I doubt Sarah would like it."

Max narrowed his eyes at her. One minute he was on the other side of the table. The next he stood in front of her, and she hadn't even seen him move. "Don't pretend to know what Sarah would have wanted. In fact, don't mention her at all."

To her disgust, Shira cowered. She threw up an arm to block the blow that had always followed harsh words. Stumbling backward, she bumped her chair and knocked it over. Max's hand shot out to steady her, but he must not have calculated the strength needed. His pull catapulted her to his chest and knocked all the wind from her lungs. She cried out.

Both his hands were on her waist, and she was sealed to him, head down and too afraid to look him in the eye to see the rage he must be feeling. When he spoke though, she was surprised by the gentleness in his tone. "I didn't mean... I wouldn't hit you."

She shook, hating her weakness. This wasn't the way to start her life over. Her hands were trapped against his chest, but she couldn't bring herself to move. They were so close, he had to feel how she trembled. He must think she was pathetic.

"Look at me."

Shira closed her eyes and pressed her lips together.

"Shira." His whisper sent chills down her spine, but not from fear. Her fingers spasmed where they lay against the hardness of his muscle and the warmth from his being. He clenched her waist a little tighter. "Look at me, Shira."

She took her time raising her head and started when her gaze met his. The deep concern she saw in his brought tears to her eyes. To her shame, they ran down her cheeks, and he made a sound in his throat before his lips covered hers. At first, Shira didn't know what to do, but then the desire she'd been feeling for him from the first time she met him rose inside her. She parted her lips to take the kiss further. He tasted so good, and his lips were soft for a man of his build. She moaned when he pushed his tongue into her mouth, but in the next instant, Max put her away from him.

His big chest rose and fell, and his breathing sounded harsh to her ears. Shira panted just as much, and she put fingers to her tingling lips. What had she been thinking going that far with the kiss? He must think she was a whore and deserved whatever treatment Sam had dealt her.

"I'm sorry," he muttered. "I couldn't think of a better way to comfort you. I made the wrong choice."

Shira frowned. "It was good. You don't have to snatch it back!"

A feather could have blown her over when Max gave a sharp bark of laughter. In a roundabout, crazy way, she had done what she set out to do.

Chapter Four

Shira tossed and turned in bed. She'd been unable to sleep since eleven. Max had left the house soon after their kiss, and he hadn't come back before she turned in for the night. Maybe she was worried about him, or it could be she wasn't used to this much country. Even in Maryland, she'd lived with Sam in the suburbs. Not far from their house had been a main thoroughfare, and one could hear traffic in the distance all hours of the night. In this house, one heard nothing except crickets. Not that she didn't like the peace. In Max's house, she had a sense of being protected, like she was cocooned from the rest of the world and specifically the danger that Sam represented.

Giving up on resting for the time being, she rose and went out to the kitchen. She didn't want to disturb the tranquility of the night, so she didn't turn on a light. The windows, barren of shades or curtains, let in plenty of moonlight, so she saw fine. A scratching toward the front of the house caught her attention, and she went to investigate. As she approached the front door, she heard it, the mewling of a cat. Shira peered out and gasped. The leopard sat on the front porch facing the house and looking right at her.

"What the hell?" Didn't anyone report to animal control around here? Then she recalled how the beast had saved her life. She owed him. The least she could do was feed him if he was hungry. She returned to the kitchen and searched the refrigerator. All the meat was frozen. She wouldn't take any out to defrost until morning. Tuna came to mind. That was cheap enough. Giving a wild animal too much of Max's food wouldn't be right. She took a can from the cabinet and opened it, and then she went back to the front door. The leopard was nowhere in sight.

Shira stood there wondering what to do. She was too scared to approach it straight out, but if it had wandered off, maybe she could leave the can out where it could find it, that would be okay. Again, she checked the window and saw that the coast was clear. She strained her ears for any sounds. None reached her except the damn crickets. Having opened the door a crack, she peeked out. She crept onto the porch and walked to the steps. She bent to put the can down and froze when she heard a sound behind her. Shira twisted in degrees to find the leopard between her and the door.

"Oh no," she squeaked. "Okay, boy, don't eat me. I have some nice tuna for you."

She slid the tuna toward the animal and waited. He sat down and watched her. Somehow he didn't appear to be threatening despite his big body and the corded muscles. After a while, the leopard lay down and actually crawled toward her. "I think I've seen it all. Did someone train you?"

He looked at her as if he was insulted. Shira covered her mouth on a chuckle. The animal ignored the tuna and lay down at her side. After a long while hesitating, she stroked his back. A muscle twitched, but he didn't move. She'd seen the same thing in a housecat she'd had once and didn't let it scare her.

"Thank you for saving me," she whispered. His ears perked each time she spoke. "I didn't think I'd get away, but you were right there. Maybe you don't remember, but Sam… He would have definitely…" Even though she spoke to an animal with no way of knowing what she was talking about, she couldn't voice the words. She hadn't spoken to anyone about how he had treated her except her mother, and that had gotten her nowhere.

"Are we going to be friends?" she asked the cat. The animal made a muffling noise and laid his head in Shira's lap. She froze in place until she realized he wasn't about to attack, and then she stroked his head. "I guess that means yes. Anyway, you better get going before Max comes back. I wouldn't want him to call animal control on you."

On impulse, she dropped a kiss on the furry head and stood. The leopard headed down the steps and walked off into the night. Shira shrugged, picked up the uneaten can of tuna, and returned to the house.

Shira decided she might as well head to bed even if she didn't think she could sleep. Funny enough, meeting the leopard must have calmed her more than she realized, because as soon as her head hit the pillow, drowsiness took hold, and she found herself drifting off.

The next time she opened her eyes, she had no idea how much time had passed. Darkness was still reflected outside her windows, and the moon had gone behind some clouds, so she couldn't see as well. Yet, she knew someone was in her room. No, not just someone. Max was in her room. She squinted at him standing just inside the door. She wondered if he'd just come home and was checking on her. He didn't know she had an animal protector now.

The longer he stood there, the more she wanted to shift her position. Her sheet had slipped low on her thighs while she slept, and she'd gone to bed in the T-shirt he'd put on her the first night. Because he hadn't purchased panties for her, she had to wash hers out, so she wore nothing under the shirt. Somehow that made her feel more naked. The only consolation was that there wasn't much light in the room, so there was no way he could see anything.

"I'm sorry for offending you earlier," she whispered.

Although she couldn't see him move, something told her she'd surprised him. "I didn't mean to wake you."

"You didn't," she lied.

"Tell me about him," he said.

She reached down for the sheet and dragged it up to her chin. The thin material seemed a poor barrier to admitting her stupidity to this man. She didn't want Max to know how weak she was, how she let Sam destroy her self-worth and rule her every waking moment for so long.

"I think you know it's painful," she said. "So I'll agree to tell you whatever you want to know, if you do the same."

She didn't have to see his face to know he frowned. At first she thought he was going to leave the room without another word, but then he pushed off the doorframe and walked over to her. He took a seat on the side of the bed, and Shira's pussy clenched as if he'd touched her.

"There's not a lot to tell. Her name was Sarah. She was my mate."

"You said that before. Is it like some biblical sense or whatever?"

"No." He didn't explain his wording but went on. "She was meant for me, and everything I could want in a partner. One day we planned to go running together. I had a last minute business deal to make and told her to wait. She needed to work off some stress, so she was looking forward to our time away from civilization."

The entire time he relayed the events from his past, he sounded emotionless and cold, like he was reporting the news, but she didn't believe he felt that way at all. The monotone was a defense mechanism.

He'd said they needed time away from civilization. Where the heck had they run, in the woods? She wouldn't put it past Max since he seemed to like his house out there in the middle of nowhere. She was a city girl. Two people couldn't be more different than she and Max. Sarah sounded like she was right down Max's alley.

"She didn't wait?" she guessed.

Max clenched a fist into the sheet, but he relaxed it right away looking at her. Shira hadn't thought to get scared.

"No, she didn't wait." He stood up and paced the room. She thought it was interesting that he didn't stumble over the ends of furniture. He must have good night vision. "She left me a voicemail that she couldn't wait. She needed time away. Her job was stressful. She was a veterinarian."

"Wow," Shira commented. His girlfriend had been a professional. She'd obviously gone to college, where Shira hadn't been able to finish. Right then, she couldn't feel more like a loser.

"There were hunters out that day." Max's tone of voice made her shiver. "They knew what they were looking for."

The way he spoke about the hunters, it seemed like the men were more than just out to shoot a deer, but she couldn't figure out what else they might be going after. Then she gasped. No, that was impossible. "Was it here or in Maine?" she asked.

"Maine, why do you ask?"

She hesitated. "Because…uh…" How could she tell him about the leopard? He'd think she was crazy, but it was a pointless explanation anyway. The beautiful cat was here in Virginia not in Maine, so there was no way they were chasing him. Although she wouldn't be surprised if the hunters wanted that cat. He seemed more intelligent than any she'd seen at the circus. Just thinking of men trying to cage him pissed her off. "No reason," she said instead.

He went on. "The hunters got her. One shot, straight to the head, which of course killed her instantly."

Shira cried out. She didn't think about it before she threw the covers aside and rose to go to him. She laid a hand on his arm and gave a light squeeze. "I'm so sorry, Max. How devastating. I can't even begin to imagine what that did to you, and to your family." Anger bubbled in her chest. "How could they even make such a stupid mistake! It's not like she looked like an animal. I saw her picture. She was pale-skinned and very beautiful."

For some reason, what she said amused him. He raised a thumb to run along her jaw line. "Thank you for that."

Shira didn't think she would ever understand the man. At the weirdest times, she made him smile. She supposed she should be happy to see it. Max took her breath away he was so sexy. His presence outweighed Sam's by a million percent, and yet she was drawn to him.

I shouldn't let myself like him too much.

They stood so close, she felt the warmth off his body. The sensation raised goose bumps along her flesh and made her too aware of how attracted she was to him. He probably didn't feel a thing, which disappointed her. To keep her head on straight, she moved back to sit on the bed and dragged the sheet over her lap.

"Like I said, I can't imagine what you went through, or what you're dealing with now but—" She bit her lip. "Max, I thought I would never climb out of the gutter I let myself get dragged into. That's the only way I can describe it, a gutter. I did climb out. Well, sort of. That's not the point. I have so much hope in me, for my future. I'm not down at all. I'm alive, and I have to believe that there's going to come a time when some seriously awesome stuff will happen, and I'm looking forward to it."

"I've never met a woman as positive as you are."

She laughed. "You mean in the face of being butt poor with no prospects?"

The sound he made had her thinking he agreed but wasn't going to admit it. "Now it's your turn."

Shira wanted to avoid the subject, but she'd set the terms of their conversation. She couldn't back down now. Unfortunately, she didn't think she could talk about her dealings with Sam in an emotionless tone like he'd done. *Just don't get to crying, girl.*

"My meeting Sam wasn't a fairytale. Well, at the time, I thought it was. I mean a doctor interested in *me*. I was a student at my local community college, starting way late, and he came there as a guest speaker. Half the women in there hung on his every word, including me. He was handsome and intelligent. After his lecture, a bunch of women ran up to him asking questions and trying to get his attention. I wasn't even trying because I figured I didn't have a chance. Later, when I was walking between buildings going to my next class, I ran into him again. I blurted out that I enjoyed what he had to say. I couldn't believe it when he ignored my comment and asked me out."

She twisted the sheet in her hands thinking back. The way Sam acted should have been a clue right there. He was never interested in what she thought or what interested her. He was all about his agenda and what he wanted.

"I was too flattered by his attention, too impressed by his credentials. I was stupid."

Max moved by the window and crossed his arms over his chest as he leaned there. "I'm sure you aren't the only woman to fall prey to that type. You shouldn't be too hard on yourself."

She sucked her teeth. "I know you're right, but it doesn't take the sting out of it."

He nodded. "Go on."

"We started dating. Like I said, everything was great, like a fairytale, but then he became more demanding, wanting to choose what I wore and who I hung out with. He couched it in compliments like, 'Honey, I care about you, so of course it's important to me that you are around the right people.' Eventually, that changed." She was pretty sure Max could figure out for himself what came next, and she didn't want to say it. Her weakness, her humiliation, wasn't easy to share. Max kept silent as if he encouraged her to go on.

In her lap, she twisted the sheet. Her fingers ached, but she kept it up. The action was the only thing to keep the tears at bay or to stop her from running out of the room. "The first time he hit me was a shock I think for both of us. He apologized. I forgave him. By then, I loved him so much. Also, my life was intertwined with his. My friends had been driven away, even my acquaintances. All of my entertainment revolved around him. He helped me to study and start getting good grades. He helped me get the better-paying job I was in at the time. Sam wanted me grateful and dependent in every way possible, and I fell for it all. So when the harsh words he sometimes spoke turned physical much more often, it was almost easy to let him do it."

She dropped her head into her hands, shoulders shaking. The sob that rose in her throat was barely contained. At any moment, she expected Max to judge her or call her pathetic, but he walked over and sat down beside her. A light touch to her leg was so warm and comforting, it set her off balance. She didn't mean to, but she found herself in his arms, leaning on his chest.

He stroked her back, and his embrace was strong and steady. She longed to stay there. Logic said she needed to get up and get distance between them. One didn't jump out of one relationship into another. Besides, he was just as emotionally damaged as she was. They didn't need to make a party of it.

"I'm sorry," she said, trying to make herself move her hands off his chest.

"Don't be." He raised her chin, and she looked into his eyes. The anger she caught there took her by surprise, but she didn't think it was directed at her. "He deserves to be castrated."

She winced but smiled. "Yeah, he does."

They stared at each other for a while, and Shira told herself to turn away, but her body didn't respond. Just the act of Max massaging a small area on her shoulder held her in place. The movement was so in contrast to the way Sam used to clench her upper arm and squeeze until he left bruises. *Yet, there's more strength one touch from Max. I can't put my finger on it. There's something different about him. What is it?*

"I should move," she whispered. Instead, she leaned in and kissed him. Her nipples brushed his chest, and Max took in a sharp breath. She nibbled his bottom lip and waited for Max to push her away, but he held very still. In degrees, she ran her hands higher on his chest until she reached his shoulders, and then she arched into him. Her body was on fire, but she shouldn't be doing this. How the heck was she trying to seduce a man like Max? This wasn't in Whisper's request to look after him, but she was turned on more than she'd ever remembered being. "Something about you…"

When he didn't move, at first she thought he wasn't interested, but all of a sudden, he swooped her up onto his lap. The sheet she'd wrapped around herself slipped, exposing her thighs. The T-shirt had risen, and her little cat was exposed. Shira shivered as Max took in the sight. She could have sworn in the dim light that his eyes changed, but he lowered his head and she couldn't see well enough.

"I shouldn't." He swallowed, still focused it seemed, on the patch between her legs. "You're a guest in my house."

"I'm actually your housekeeper," she corrected.

"All the more reason not to...*do* what we both have in mind."

Of course, I'm the hired help. "I get it." She slipped off of his lap and stood yanking the T-shirt down.

Max rose. "Make no mistake about it. I want you, but it's a been a long time since I was with anyone."

She waved a hand but kept her eyes averted. "Oh yeah, of course. Don't even worry about it. I completely understand."

He strolled to the door and was gone before she drew her next breath. Bitter regret choked her and made her drop into bed knowing it would be a long time before she slept.

Chapter Five

To Shira's annoyance, Max avoided her for most of the next few days. He didn't stick around the house much, and even when he did, he spent most of the time out in the shed tinkering with she didn't know what. Shira busied herself with cleaning and re-cleaning the house. She experimented with various recipes, some of which she was able to download off the Internet using his laptop.

Once she met him in the hall and blocked his path. She knew she looked a hot mess with wrinkled, damp clothes, but she didn't appreciate his attitude. "So you're scared of me. Is that it?"

Max's eyebrows went up. He studied her from head to toe, and the words she'd blurted out embarrassed her. She didn't weigh much on a good day, and he must be just over two hundred pounds of solid muscle. "Scared? No." Max put a thumb up and rubbed it across her cheek. "You're dirty."

"Thanks," she snapped. "If you weren't such a slob, I wouldn't be."

Amusement lit his eyes. "If I were a neat freak, I might not need you."

"Seriously!" She huffed and turned to walk away, but he caught her arm and swung her around. Shira found herself penned to the wall, and Max's big frame keeping her there. The emotions roiling to the surface were both surprise and desire. He glared at her for a long while, saying nothing. Shira couldn't catch her breath to protest, or for that matter to encourage him.

He dipped his head so that his mouth came close to hers. Her lips parted of their own accord, but he didn't take the invitation. "Is this what you wanted?"

"I..." Her brain was scrambled.

"You play a dangerous game, little girl," he warned. "You do not want to tempt the beast."

"Interesting choice of words," she quipped.

His eyes narrowed. "Why is that?"

"Nothing." She lowered her gaze. He didn't need to know about the leopard, but then it didn't have anything to do with him anyway. "Are you going to start something or let me go?"

Max released her too quickly and stepped back. "I'll stay out of your way. It's better for both of us."

Shira decided not to argue. She might not be Max's first choice of a partner, but he was attracted to her. The bulge she'd felt in his pants when he pressed her to the wall said it. That was enough to stroke even her tiny ego. She smiled as she headed down the hall, and Max kept going in the opposite direction.

Sometime later, Shira was just finishing up with drying the dinner dishes when one of the glasses slipped from her hand shattered on the floor. She swore, hoping Max wouldn't be too angry.

"Leave it. I'll pick it up," he said from the doorway.

She gasped. She'd thought he'd gone back outside after he ate. "No, I'm sorry. I'll get it up in a jiffy." She stooped and picked up the first piece a little too quickly. A sharp pain sliced through her palm. "Damn."

Max was there in a flash. "Let me see."

"It's fine." She tried pulling away from him, but he held her wrist in a firm grip.

He concentrated on the cut, and Shira cringed at the gush of blood that welled up and fell in great glops onto the floor she'd scrubbed earlier. Max hauled her to her feet and guided her to the sink. While he stood behind her he washed her hand under cool water. Only the pain could keep her from enjoying his closeness.

"This looks deep," he said. "I think you'll need stitches. I'll take you to the hospital."

"No!"

"That wasn't a suggestion."

Shira snatched her hand away, grabbed a wad of paper towels, and wound them around her palm. "I said it's fine. I'm not going to the hospital."

His nostrils flared. "And *I* said you're going. You will not bleed to death in my house."

"Be still my heart," she groused. "I didn't know you cared so much."

Shira's smartass comments covered the fact that dread had risen with the mention of the hospital. She couldn't go there, not with the risk of running into Sam. She spun on her heel and started for the kitchen door. Max caught up with her and grabbed her elbow. She couldn't get away from him without a fight, so she headed outside and let him open the car door for her to get in. Down the highway, she sat like a statue beside him, saying nothing. As she watched more and more of the tissue turning red, she had to admit Max was right. She needed stitches.

"Put pressure on it, and raise your arm. That should slow down the flow."

She did as he suggested. "I…I don't have any money or ID."

"I'll take care of it."

"I don't know why I didn't think of that before." She had, but somehow she'd felt safe hidden away at his house. The fact that they were heading back to civilization and possibly Sam was a wake up call. Waiting until she'd saved enough money might not be an option. She would need to ask Max for help getting new ID. Then she would go, money or no money.

The moment they pulled into the hospital parking lot, her jaw started hurting from clenching it so tight, and her head pounded. The one consolation she had was that any emotion in her expression Max would probably put down to the pain in her hand, which had dulled to a slight ache.

He opened her door and guided her into the emergency room entrance. *Please don't be on duty. Please don't be on duty.*

When they passed through the sliding glass doors, Max had pulled out ahead of her by the fact that he had longer legs and wasn't lagging in dread like she was. He stopped cold though, and she smashed into his back. Grumbling, Shira moved from behind him and glanced up. Max drew in a sharp, swift breath like he smelled something foul. Rage transformed his handsome face.

Shira stumbled in nervous fear and took a step back, but he reached for her and walked alongside her to the triage nurse's station. She listened in a daze as Max commanded attention, gave his personal information, and had a nurse evaluating her cut in seconds.

"You'll have to wait here, sir, if—"

Max cut her off. "I am her fiancé. I'm going back."

Shira's mouth dropped open. She should probably tell him it wasn't necessary to join her since all she was getting was a shot and stitches, neither of which she was scared of. The truth was, she was nervous about running into Sam. He wasn't likely to attack at work, but still, she was scared.

With her good hand, Shira held onto Max's arm. She told herself over and over to "woman up" and stand on her own, but her fingers wouldn't uncurl from his sleeve. Max made no mention of it. In fact, she wondered if he knew she stood at his side the way he swung his gaze from one face to another as they walked, like he searched for someone. Her stomach clenched. Did he remember her saying Sam was a doctor? No, even if he did, there was no reason for him to think he worked in emergency medicine. Virginia was a big enough state, and there were plenty of hospitals for Sam to work in. Only she knew that this one happened to be where he'd taken a position.

They were led into a curtained off section, and Shira took a seat. Max stood near the hall, arms crossed, alert. She chewed her lip. "Max, what's wrong?"

He frowned. "Nothing."

Was he always like this in hospitals? Was he afraid like she was but for a different reason? She wondered if the last time he'd been in the emergency room was when his girlfriend died. Maybe that's what was upsetting him. Thinking that turned her mind from her own issues, and she searched for some way to soothe him.

"It's fine. Everything is okay, Max," she said.

He gave her a look full of curiosity, and then the curtain slid back. Shira almost vomited and fainted on the floor. She sucked in a deep, steadying breath that did absolutely nothing for her.

"Shira, what a surprise," Sam said, but he didn't look surprised at all. She knew he'd read the chart with her name on it and made sure to rush over—any opportunity to make her life miserable.

"S-Sam," she whispered and then cleared her throat.

"*You're* the doctor?" Max asked. She couldn't believe the hostility in his tone. One would have thought he knew Sam was her ex, but he couldn't know that. The only one who would was that leopard that had stopped him from dragging her back into his car that rainy night.

"I am." Sam gave a blinding smile that she used to watch him practice in the mirror when he wanted to impress. The act fell flat with Max, and Sam frowned a little before he recovered himself. "I'm Doctor Samuel Ellerby. Shira is an old friend of mine, and it's good seeing her. You are?"

He offered his hand to shake Max's, but Max ignored it.

"My employer," Shira rushed to say, but she didn't know why. Maybe it was the fact that Sam intimidated her.

Max glanced at her, but he didn't contradict what she said. Sam seemed too pleased, and she kicked herself for not going with Max's earlier excuse, that he was her fiancé. Of course Sam wouldn't believe that knowing how recently they were together, but she could have let him think she and Max were involved. Max outweighed him by a good thirty pounds and was taller by several inches. The wildness she'd sensed in Max when she met him was plain even in his leaning against the wall unmoving. Watching him and knowing he would protect her if need be calmed her down some.

"Then maybe I'll need to see my patient while you wait in the visitor's area?" Sam suggested.

"No."

Both Shira and Sam blinked at his one word answer with no pretense of being pleasant. Shira put a hand to her mouth and tried not to laugh at the reddening, which started in Sam's cheeks. She liked Max a lot!

"No?" Sam stuttered with a few incomprehensible words before he turned to Shira. In the past, if she'd reduced him to idiot status, she would have paid for it with tears and pain. She was glad Max was the one dishing it out. Let him try getting into her boss's face. He could see what he got.

With an expression of innocence, Shira held her hand out to Sam. She didn't want to trust him to stitch her up, but he wouldn't risk his livelihood just to get back at her. He ground his teeth together so obviously, she was surprised she didn't hear the noise. After he'd washed his hands and had a nurse assist him with numbing her, he eventually stitched her up. By the time they were ready to leave, Shira was on cloud nine. All she'd done to escape Sam was worth it. Going to Max was a good choice. Her hope in the future multiplied tenfold.

When they were almost out the door leading to the waiting area, a nurse stopped them. "I'm sorry Mr. Macgregor, I have a form I forgot to have you sign."

Max paused. "Sure."

The nurse started to walk away, and Max followed. Shira yawned. She stayed near the door, leaning against the wall and thinking about the rest of the mess she needed to clean up at home. She hadn't realized she closed her eyes until she sensed someone nearby. She popped upright and started to find Sam in front of her.

Shira shifted left to see if she saw Max, but he was nowhere in sight. Sam moved to block her view. "What's between you two?"

"Nothing," she muttered. "If you'll excuse me." She started to go around him, but he blocked her path once again.

"Do you think he's going to keep you from me?"

The pounding in her head, which had calmed since they arrived, started up again. She didn't answer.

"You belong to me, Shira, until I'm ready to toss you aside," Sam warned her. "I'm going to bring you home, and you're going to pay for ever having anything to do with him."

Shira balled her hands into fists. "Back off! I'm over you. You can't scare me anymore, Sam. I'm never returning to your house or having anything to do with you."

He chuckled low in his throat so that it sounded menacing. Shira didn't want to admit that it scared the crap out of her. "You know the influence I have, the people I know. How long do you think he'll tolerate you after I ruin his life?"

"Y-You wouldn't do that." She cursed herself. "He's not some nobody that you can push around with your money."

Sam's grin widened, and he raised an eyebrow. "Oh? You've got me curious, Shira. Just who is this guy? Something tells me he's more than just your boss. What kind of service do you provide for him?"

She shook with anger and fear. Instead of getting Sam to drop his interest in her, she'd only whetted his appetite, making him want to know more about Max. Hell, she didn't know much about the man. What she did had been enough. He was a good man, and he didn't deserve Sam's acid directed at him. The sooner she got out of town the better.

***

Max scratched his name on the last line of paperwork. He didn't know why, but he felt like this stupid nurse found extra forms for him to sign that weren't necessary. At first he suspected she was interested in him, but she didn't do any of the things he'd come to recognize in women who were attracted to him. Of course he scented it on her, but it wasn't for him.

He paused over the last sheet. "What do you think of Doctor Ellerby?" he asked.

The blue eyes turned cloudy, and a simpering grin stretched her deep rose lips. "He's brilliant! I can't believe we have such a great man at our hospital. When we met him..."

Max didn't need to listen to more. Now he knew the truth. That bastard had asked this airhead to distract him so he could get at Shira. *If he's upset her, I will shred him!*

Shoving the papers at the nurse, he turned away and ignored her calls saying she had one more. As he walked toward the area where he'd left Shira, he drew in a deep breath. He didn't need to get this worked up over a human woman. She wasn't his type, and he had no intention of taking their relationship any further than it's already inappropriate state. He knew they were more than employer and employee. Hell, they were practically living a role-playing fantasy, but that's all it could be—without the sex.

Well, the guy's an asshole, so I can still wipe the floor with him, he mused. The minute they walked into the hospital earlier, he'd picked up on the scent. He recognized it from that night in the rain when he had stopped Ellerby from dragging Shira into his car. He had realized later from her sharing of her past that the man wasn't just some random pervert. He was her ex. Too bad he hadn't also made the connection that she didn't want to go to the hospital because he worked there. The fact that Ellerby was an emergency room doctor hadn't entered his mind.

Max picked up his step when he spotted Ellerby talking to Shira in a low tone near the exit. Max stopped behind him. "You have nothing to say to her," he growled. "Get lost."

He raised his hand to snatch the doctor by the collar and drag him away, but Shira darted around him and grabbed his arm. "It's fine, Max. Let's go."

Max didn't move. He flared his nostrils and stared into Ellerby's face. Everything inside of him wanted to attack. The beast was coiled for it, but this wasn't the time or the place. He didn't make a habit of going after humans even if they deserved it, and not since he'd visited Whisper in his leopard form did he risk exposure. He'd been unable to resist visiting Shira in his shifted form. Of course, he'd told himself it was just boredom that drove him, but deep inside he wanted to see how she would act. After all she'd been through, he should have thought twice about risking her fear. He was an idiot.

Shira tugged on his arm again, pulling him from his thoughts. "Max."

He shook himself and nodded. While they drove back to his house, he watched her from the corner of his eye. Shira was afraid, and the realization enraged him. He tightened his hands on the steering wheel and did all he could not to swing the car around and drive back to the hospital.

"What did he say to you?" he asked.

She squirmed in her seat. "Nothing."

"You're lying to me."

"It doesn't matter, Max. Let it go. Sam is in my past, and I'm not letting him get to me." She offered him a smile that was obviously forced. "I've moved on, and I'm happy."

"You *were* happy at my house." He left the comment at that because he regretted saying it. He'd spoken the truth though. Shira had hidden away, and he didn't mind. She'd needed time from civilization, from the man that hurt her and from the knowledge that her choices had kept her in the situation as long as she'd been in it. He knew she blamed herself in that respect. Yet, the blame should be placed like a boulder on the head of that fool. "I'll leave it for now, but don't let him get to you.

He is a weak, small man, and he will not come against me or anyone in my care if he knows what's good for him."

Shira sat in silence with her head bowed. After some time, she whispered, "Thank you. You're a good person, but I don't want to drag you into my mess. I…just thanks, for everything."

Max didn't push, but an inflection in her words gave him a sense of finality. A suspicion rose inside of him, but he kept his thoughts to himself and continued the drive home.

Chapter Six

The night had grown late, and Shira stayed in bed as long as she could. She kept falling asleep because her mind and body were worn out. One would think she couldn't rest after Sam's threats. She had bid Max goodnight after they got home and cleaned up the mess in the kitchen. Or rather he'd cleaned it up. He hadn't let her cross the threshold. In the end, she had told him she was going to bed, but she kept her clothes on in preparation of leaving when he fell asleep.

Of course going this way was ridiculous. All she had to do was say it wasn't working out and she had to move on. Somehow she didn't want to face Max and see him work out the truth about why she'd come to this decision—that she was scared. If he questioned her, she feared he'd learn about the specific threat to his life Sam had made. No, she had to go in the middle of the night. That was her only option and best for everyone.

She threw her legs over the side of the bed and reached beneath it for her shoes. After putting them on, she tiptoed to the bedroom door and listened. Max slept like the dead, she had learned. The man didn't even snore, and he kept his bedroom door open as if he liked being ready at a moment's notice. She had at first worried that could be a problem in passing his room, but then she remembered the window of one of the guest rooms was the single place no bush had been planted beneath. The house was a rancher, so she could climb out and drop to the ground.

As she gathered her bag, guilt assailed her. Max had given her money the day before, way more than she needed to get incidentals like pads or for that matter the underwear she still needed. He'd promised to take her to the store in the morning, but that wouldn't be necessary. She would leave this area long behind. In fact, she would leave Virginia in her wake.

The money wasn't enough to start a new life, but somehow she would find a way to live. There were shelters and other opportunities. People found a leg up out of the gutter every day. So would she.

Shira eased her bedroom door open, paused to listen, and then inched into the hall. Each step she took was excruciating, but there were no sounds from Max's room. She made it into the spare bedroom, still empty of furniture. That was a good thing. At least she wouldn't crack her knee on the edge of a dresser or bed frame.

The window latch opened without a hitch, and the window rose. She was glad she'd come in here to dust the windowsill, so she wouldn't sneeze and give herself away. She peered out through the window and wondered how she would coordinate the climb with her bandaged hand. She didn't want to bust her stiches.

"Can I help you onto the sill?" came the deep voice from behind her.

Shira froze. "*Fuck!*"

Max tsked. "Such language."

She turned slowly from the window, and he strode toward her. She was a deer caught in headlights. The expression was old but so apt about then. Max stopped just to her left, leaned forward to close the window, and faced her. "What were you doing?"

She frowned and folded her arms. "You know what I was doing." Her bag lay on the floor not far from his feet. He eyed it with a raised brow, and she fought the need to defend herself. "It's for the best."

"Whose best? Yours? Mine? You mean for you to sneak out of the house in the middle of the night?"

"Nobody was sneaking," she snapped.

She started to walk off, but he stepped into her path and stood as solid as a tree. If she wanted to get through him, she'd have to bring a lot more strength than she possessed. All of a sudden, her palm itched to smack his face because something told her he'd been awake the entire time, waiting for her to make a move.

"You can't keep me here, Max."

"I wouldn't dream of it."

She grunted, frustrated that he spoke so deadpan, like they discussed the weather.

"You're letting him run you out of town like a scared little girl, and I'm calling you on it. How is that holding you prisoner?"

Crack! She'd done it before she knew she would follow through, and she gasped in horror. Even in the moonlight, she saw his eyes change and the anger that filled them. She took a step back only to crash into the wall.

"I'm so sorry. Please don't…"

He pivoted and presented a broad back to her. "If you want to pretend you're starting over by letting him chase you away, be my guest."

He walked toward the door, but she ran after him. "You don't know anything about it. Who's the last person that bullied you, huh? How many punches have put you on the floor trying to draw a breath but can't because it burns so bad? How many times have you been told you're so disgustingly thin you look like a boy?"

To her horror and shame, she started to cry, and she would have run past Max to hide in her room if he didn't catch her. She fought him, pounding at his shoulders and kicking his shins. He wouldn't let go.

"Stop it, Shira, before you bust your stitches."

"What the hell do you care?" she griped.

He hoisted her off her feet and carried her across the hall to her room. She struggled against him the entire way, but he didn't release her until he dropped her on her bed. Shira was about to scramble to the other side until he joined her. She froze in shock, staring at him stretched with casual grace on a bed she realized was too small for his large frame. His presence made her feel tiny, but no longer afraid. In fact she couldn't believe how her anger and despair had morphed to desire without warning.

Max ran a palm over her hair, brushing it from her face. She didn't move. "He is both a fool and a liar." She looked away, but Max grasped her chin and made her look at him. "You know you're beautiful, don't you?"

"Don't say what you don't mean."

"I never do."

His hand went from her chin to the space between her breasts. Even though he didn't touch her nipples, he might as well have. They grew taut in anticipation, but he moved on, skimming her belly and lower to the zipper on her pants. Shira's breath caught in her throat. 'You don't have to prove anything."

"Tell me not to touch you, and I won't."

How the hell was she going to say that? She wanted it all right. She wanted it *bad*. Horny didn't exist the way it did now, until after she'd met Max. When she didn't deny it, he ran his hand lower still, and Shira arched her back the second his hand settled between her legs. A gentle squeeze sent pleasure to every corner of her being. She pushed her ass into the bed and brought her hips up to meet his touch. He curled his fingers until only one was straight to torment her. Max flicked the single digit over her swelling bud through her clothes, and she bit off a moan.

Would he go all the way this time, or would he back off? Was he doing this to prove that he thought she was beautiful, or to convince her that she was, no matter what he thought? Her mind raced with questions, and yet, all she wanted was to forget the reasons and let it happen. *If* it did.

She rolled onto her side toward him and ran a palm over his chest. Max's hand stilled, which she'd trapped between her legs. "Do you really want me?"

He looked down, and she followed his line of sight. The bulge in his pants was unbelievable, and her mouth watered. Just how big was he? Daring to see for herself, she did as he had done, moving her hand down his chest. Max's abs clenched beneath her touch. He'd removed his T-shirt earlier, so she got a good look at the perfection of his upper body. Rippling muscle responded each spot her fingers skimmed, and she took her time exploring. When she reached the band of his boxers, she paused, waiting for him to protest. This time he must be serious, because she knew from past relationships, play with a man's cock, and there was no turning back without major disappointment.

She curled her fingers inside the band and dragged it lower. A trimmed patch of blond hair came into view. She licked her lips and swallowed. When she peered up at him, she caught the excitement in the dark depths of his eyes. Max was in it, and although he seemed like a very dominant man, he was letting her enjoy herself while he waited. For some reason, that knowledge choked her up. Sam had rolled her onto her back and penetrated her before she could catch her breath.

She uncovered Max's cock and swore in amazement. The man was hung. She almost wanted to pay homage to the long, thick shaft. A brief touch with the tips of two fingers let her know it was hard as a rock. Shira didn't ask for permission. She couldn't help reaching in and stroking it from base to tip. The shaft responded to her touch, twitching under her hand. She straightened her fingers and ran them all the way down to his balls, massaged there a moment, and headed back to the top. The head dripped with precome, and she teased it with a light touch.

"Mm, Shira," Max moaned.

She looked at him again. "Are you going to give me some of this?"

"Do you want some?"

"Ya think?"

He chuckled at her smart mouth but removed her hand from his dick. Shira could have sobbed in regret. "I'm not saying no, but I want to be sure you're not in too much pain."

"I'm doped up," she insisted.

He caught her injured hand and looked at it. Her bandages were snug, and she'd been given painkillers. She'd taken another one not too long ago, so she was good. Besides, the wound wasn't so bad now.

Max appeared doubtful. "I don't want to be selfish."

She leaned back and raised her T-shirt a bit, exposing her belly. A little higher and the edge of her bra was revealed. She was small, but her breasts were perky with good size nipples. She could go without a bra but didn't often because of them. "If you don't want it, I understand."

She made a show of unbuttoning her jeans and then lowering the zipper. Max's exposed cock seemed to strain toward her. "I never said that."

He flipped her onto her back and moved above her. "Did I not warn you about teasing me?" She matched the grin on his face with one of her own. Not even a good two weeks ago, it was as if he never smiled, but she could bring one to his lips no problem now. Pride swelled inside of her, and she wondered what else she could do for him. "What is that look for?" he demanded.

She shrugged. "I don't know."

He hadn't brought his weight down on her, so she had room to flip over, and she did, sticking her ass up until it brushed his crotch. Max moaned.

"Damn it, woman, we shouldn't do this."

"Why not?" She pushed her jeans over her hips, exposing her panties. "These are the only panties I have. I really should take them off before you make me ruin them."

"I'm sorry. I should have bought you more by now. I didn't want to presume."

She sucked her teeth. "Please, you saw no reason not to choose my clothes. Why not my panties?" She glanced at him over her shoulder. His gaze was directed at her ass. Shira bit her lip. Max wasn't fooling anybody. He hadn't bought panties for her because it meant shopping in the middle of some really sexy stuff, and at the time, he didn't intend on giving into the attraction between them. Well, she wasn't taking no for an answer this time. Should or shouldn't, they were grown, and she wanted to see what it was like to be in the arms of a man like him.

She rose to her knees, and as she did, he backed up some as if he was scared to let his skin touch hers. She noted he didn't bother tucking his cock away though. Shira shed her clothing with her back still turned to him. Her bra and panties landed on the floor behind the T-shirt and jeans, and then she laid an arm over her breasts to glance at him.

Now that she was naked, nerves kicked in. She was underweight, although she was pretty sure she'd put on a few pounds being in Max's house and eating with him. If she didn't see desire flaming to life in his eyes, she didn't know how she would live down the embarrassment. *Well, he said it's been a while.*

He laid a tentative hand on her back and stroked. "You're so small. I feel like I'll crush you."

"I'm durable." She reached behind her and grabbed hold of his cock. Rubbing it over her ass cheek and moaning made his member twitch in her hold. She gave it a small squeeze and then guided it between her legs to push back on it. Max's cock didn't enter her, but just the act of them going all the way seemed to set him off.

"Shira, damn it, I need…" He cut himself off, but she knew what he wanted to say. She lay down on the pillow while pushing her ass high in the air. She ran palms over his hard thighs and wiggled her hips. A growl erupted from Max's throat that startled her at first, but she decided it was just the heat of the moment and the blood rushing through her ears that made her think the noise was more animal than human.

"Aren't you going to put that in me, Max?" she teased, speaking in a deep, throaty tone. "You don't want me to suffer, do you?"

"Hell, no."

She smiled at his passion. Max leaned down and kissed her ass cheek. Shira's pussy clenched. She gripped the sheets until her fingers ached but waited for him to make the next move. When he bent and ran his tongue along her heated skin, she thought she'd lose it. Max planted kiss after kiss and followed them with more licks. Just the fact that he was back there doing what he was doing had her shaking from head to toe.

"Max, I think…" What did she think? She had no idea. Did she want him to stop or something? Her mind wasn't acting right. She couldn't figure out what she should say let alone what he should do. The one thing that started to become clear was that she didn't want him to stop touching her. Her body was hot and ready to ignite at any second. The only man to put the fire out was Max because he had started it. "I want it."

""Right here?" He kissed her so close to her back entrance, she yelped in alarm and excitement.

"Um." She was too scared to admit what she wanted.

"Tell me, Shira." He kissed her closer to the entrance. Tremors rippled through her thighs.

"W-Whatever you want," she said, coping out.

"Oh no you don't." He nipped the back of her thigh, and she cried out. He soothed the spot with a lick of that big, rough tongue. Then he bit her again. Goose bumps broke out on her arms and legs. Strength ebbed until she thought she'd collapse on the bed. "Maybe you want it here."

Max shoved her cheeks apart and sucked so hard on her juicy pussy that she screamed in delight. "Yes!"

"Ah, there's an answer." He went at her again, this time sticking his tongue inside. Shira whimpered and pushed against his mouth. He slurped and licked until the sounds and the feel drove her to the brink. Her inner muscles clenched. She scratched at the bed. An orgasm threatened to take hold, and she gave into it, pleading for him not to stop.

Over and over he ate her. Shira whispered his name, both excited that he was so into making her feel good and nervous that he would draw away before she was done. Her body was greedy for more. Each time he brought her to climax, she craved another.

"I'm being selfish," she muttered, gasping for breath. "You should get yours."

"Mm," he moaned, allowing the vibrations to tickle her overstimulated pussy. "Do you think I'm not enjoying you? Do you know how sweet your come is?"

"I don't know." She moaned as an orgasm took hold. When the tidal wave of pleasure eased, he sat up. Shira was about to turn around, but Max held her still. He moved in behind her, and she arched her back. She was so wet and ready. From the first penetration of his massive cock, she stiffened.

"No, sweetheart, relax," he instructed.

She sucked in a deep breath and let it out slowly. None of her previous lovers had been so well-endowed. Max didn't hurt her. He seemed to be taking his time, waiting for her muscles to relax, but he stretched her. She felt so full, it overwhelmed her and sapped her energy.

Max squeezed her hip and massaged it with a gentleness that didn't surprise her. "I don't want to hurt you. It's hard to hold on. It's been so long."

"I know." She covered his hand. "You're not hurting me. It feels good."

To show him she wasn't afraid or worried, she began pumping her hips, making it so his cock slipped deep inside of her and then out to the tip. The sensation was incredible, and from the way Max panted, she knew he felt the same. He hadn't begun to move yet. From what she'd learned about him so far, she was pretty sure it would piss him off if he released too early.

Neither of them had anything to worry about because Max gained control of his body, and when he did, he held her in an iron grip without pain. He arched his hips to push his cock to the hilt, and then he pulled out until not even his head pierced her. Shira grunted in complaint, but Max set the pace. He placed his cock tip against her pussy. She tried pushing onto it, but he wouldn't let her move.

"Hold still," he commanded.

"Put it in me," she pleaded.

He teased her pussy from base to top and twirled the head of his cock over her bud. Shira cried out his name. He dipped the head into her put pulled out too quickly. She smacked his thigh, and he drove into her hard and deep.

"Yes, yes," she encouraged him. "Take all of me, Max."

"I intend to."

He thrust so fast and hard over and over, but the movements were controlled to the point that he didn't bump her cervix or cause her any pain. Her muscles stretched around his girth, yet they sucked at him as well, eager to be invaded. Shira rotated her hips the best she could.

"Max, I want to pump," she begged.

He whipped out of her and rolled them both to the end of the bed. Shira found herself sitting on his lap facing him, and he entered her. She held onto his shoulders while he grasped her hips. "Do it," he encouraged her.

Shira began bouncing up and down his length. She arched into his chest, and each time she rose or fell, her taut nipples scraped his chest and sent missiles of pleasure to her pussy. She called out his name, and he shouted hers. They found each other's mouths, and Shira pushed her tongue between his lips. She couldn't get enough. Her libido was high, but Max's seemed to be a good match.

"Please tell me you can keep this up all night," she pleaded.

The growl she heard this time couldn't be mistaken—definitely animal. She didn't give a damn as long as Max ravished her and she could come again.

"I will take you as long as you can handle me," he told her. "Make no mistake about it—you will beg me to stop before I am done."

Shira squeezed her legs around his waist. "You're on!"

Chapter Seven

Shira woke up to her hand killing her. If her stitches weren't busted under the bandages, she'd be surprised. Not once in their all night sex party had she thought of the injury, but now it could not be ignored. She climbed out of bed and went to the bathroom. Max wasn't beside her when she opened her eyes. He was an early riser, yet he didn't mind eating breakfast late. Only at that moment, looking at herself in the bathroom mirror, did she realize they had fallen into a routine over the last couple of weeks.

She grinned. "Damn, I almost look like a woman in love."

Shira shook her head. No way. Too soon. Max would be a rebound relationship, so it couldn't go anywhere. As she brushed her teeth, flossed, and used mouthwash, she wondered what he thought of them having sex the night before. *I just hope he'll want a repeat as often as possible.*

After she was dressed, she headed toward the kitchen, checking rooms to see if she spotted Max. He was nowhere in sight. When she got to the kitchen, she noted the sheet of paper there, and a flutter stirred in her chest. *Get a grip, Shira. You're not in love, girl.* She thought the words in a sing-songy tone that did nothing to help her pull it together.

The note was short and without emotion:

> *Needed to go to the bank. We will make arrangements about where you'll go when I get back. Do not leave before then.*
> *- Max*

Shira sank into a chair, glad it was behind her because she hadn't checked before her knees gave out. All the giddiness of a moment ago drained away. Whatever she'd thought about last night was *not* how Max saw it. He was, under no circumstances, in love. To her bitter disappointment and shame, tears welled up in her eyes and spilled down her cheeks.

Of course she couldn't blame him. After all, she'd been trying to convince herself from the beginning. A man like Max Macgregor didn't choose a woman like her to be with long term. He was on another level. The sex had been good. She knew he'd enjoyed himself, but that was it. Shira could feel good that she had brought him out of his funk and helped him to smile. He had protected her, and it sounded like he wanted to help get her on her feet so she could leave town. She should sit here and be grateful, happy even.

While she sat there feeling sorry for herself, the doorbell rang. She sniffed and found tissue to wipe her nose. No one ever visited, and as far as she knew Max hadn't ordered more furniture. Not that he was forthcoming about his plans. The note he'd left had been a surprise, but then he didn't want her to leave and feel guilty. She told herself that to try to cheer up. The argument didn't work.

Shira peeped out the window and gasped when she saw Whisper. The woman looked exactly the same as she'd been the last time Shira had seen her. Behind her old schoolmate stood a man comparable in height and build to Max. In fact, he couldn't be anyone else but Max's twin.

Shira unlocked the door and jerked it open. "Oh my goodness, Whisper!"

"Shira," Whisper shrieked and ran into Shira's arms. They hugged laughing. "I can't believe how little you've changed, girl. What's it been, fifteen years?"

"About that." She stepped back and let them both in. "I'm sorry Max isn't in. He had a couple of errands to run."

Whisper waved her hand and moved into the living room. She

studied the room, and Shira remembered that she hadn't seen the furniture before. Probably the last time she'd been to Max's house, the place had been empty.

"Oh, wow, this looks awesome. I like what you've done with the place."

Shira shifted from one foot to the other and picked at her pants leg. "Not my doing. Max chose his own furniture. I'm just the help."

Whisper rolled her eyes. "Don't you talk like that. The fact that he let you stay here is a lot. Trust me."

Shira felt eyes on her, and she turned to find Max's brother's piercing gaze trained in her direction. Her throat was dry, and she swallowed, but nothing helped. The same sense of danger rolled off this man, but she couldn't read him the way she felt like she could read Max. Plus his darker looks made him seem more mysterious. She wasn't sure she liked him.

"Where are my manners," Whisper chirped. "This is my boyfriend, Alec. He's Max's twin."

Shira muttered a greeting. She didn't remember Whisper being so bouncy. Being in love must suit her big time. Jealousy was an ugly beast, so she beat it down and forced a smile.

"How are you?" Alec held his hand out, and she shook it but then put distance between them.

"Would you two like something to eat?" she offered. "I know it's close to lunch time, but I haven't eaten, and I feel like I'm about to pass out."

Whisper linked her arm with hers. "I'm famished."

"You wouldn't be if you weren't in such a hurry to get back to Virginia," Alec complained. Whisper ignored him and all but dragged Shira off in the direction of the kitchen.

Shira hesitated as she took eggs, bacon, and sausage from the refrigerator. "Is everything okay? I thought you told me you'd be back in about a month."

Whisper shuddered. "Girl, I was done with those people. You wouldn't believe the amount of testosterone thrown around up there. Everything was a contest, and Alec has so many male cousins feeling themselves it's ridiculous. Of course they were all sexy as hell, but Alec gets a little overprotective and…well, never mind. We're home. Let me help you cook."

They worked together talking about old times in high school. Shira enjoyed the female companionship. She hadn't had a friend in forever, and the way Whisper took to her, she wondered if the woman didn't feel the same. Regret stirred her heart thinking soon she would be gone.

"What about you?" Whisper said, a question Shira had been dreading. "You said you came by my apartment looking for me when you met Max. Is everything okay?"

Shira didn't want to discuss it, but she owed Whisper an explanation. Whisper had vouched for Max, and because she was an old friend, he had given Shira a job and a place to stay. With as few words as possible and stuffing her emotions down, she told Whisper about Sam. The anger that sparked in the woman's eyes surprised her.

"He should have his dick cut off."

Shira burst out laughing, and her friend joined her. "You're right. He should. Well, I'm free now, and I'm never going back. I'm going to make something of my life and see my dreams come true."

"Good for you!" Whisper hugged her. "Now let's get this food on because Alec didn't say but he's hungry, and he's a big grump when his stomach is empty."

Shira shook her head. "Does he eat like an animal, because Max sure does."

Whisper started as if Shira had surprised her, but she smiled. "Yeah, like an animal."

Just when they were setting a huge bowl of scrambled eggs, a platter of pancakes, and another of bacon and sausage on the table, a key sounded in the front door. Shira's hand shook, and Alec nabbed the pitcher of ice tea she still held. She couldn't help her gaze arrowing straight to Max when he walked into the room. His focused on her as well, but then he shifted his attention to his brother.

"Hey," he said.

"Hey, yourself." Alec walked over to him and shook his hand. Whisper elbowed past the big man and threw herself into Max's arms.

"Max! It's good to see you," she said. "Although I admit I thought you'd be looking less grumpy since Shira is here."

"Can you be less obvious?" he complained. "I had enough of your matchmaking before you left, woman."

Shira watched their interaction. They joked and prodded each other. When Whisper went into his arms, he hugged her tight and kissed the top of her head. Again jealousy rose in Shira's chest. She tamped it down and turned to the table.

"You're just in time to eat," she said.

"Good," he responded.

They all sat down, and Shira remained quiet while Max and his brother chatted about family. Occasionally, Whisper tossed in an observation about whomever they were discussing. Shira shoveled her food around her plate, not hungry. She'd never felt so out of place, like she didn't belong. Max had gone out that morning to get money so he could get her going on her way. She couldn't blame him. After all, she'd been about to leave in the middle of the night. Yet, deep inside, she'd hoped he would ask her to stay. Pride wouldn't let her beg. He didn't want her.

"I was wondering, Whisper," she blurted, cutting off their conversation. She ducked her head when they all turned her way, and then forced it up. "Do you mind if I crash at your place a short while? I promise it won't be long, just until I find a job and I can stand on my own two feet."

No one said a word, but Shira started a little at the clatter of Max dropping his fork on his plate. He rushed to pick it up, and then set it down again. From the tension she caught in his shoulders and the way he had clenched the utensils, she knew he was angry. So what? He was the one that left her a note like them having sex meant diddly.

"You have a job," Max snapped.

She frowned. "A temporary one, and if I'm not mistaken, it was ending today!"

"That wasn't settled."

She turned to Whisper. "I can come here from your place every morning, and leave in the evening to go back. Is it okay?"

Whisper hesitated. Her glance swung from Shira to Max. "Of course, girl, no problem. I've spent most of my time at Alec's house, but I'll be glad to stay with you and help you get back on point. It'll be fun."

"I thought you were moving in permanently, Whisper," Alec interjected. "We discussed it."

"Right, we talked about it," Whisper agreed. "I never said one way or another."

"You can stay here a little longer," Max said.

Shira rolled her eyes. "Yeah, I think I'll be fine at Whisper's."

He grumbled. Shira didn't know why he had a problem with it. Not like he really wanted her to stay. Maybe his issue was that he didn't arrange the solution. She didn't give a fat rat's ass.

Whisper and Alec began arguing about her living arrangements, and guilt assailed Shira. She would tell her she didn't have to stay at the apartment with her. Shira would be fine on her own.

Max picked his fork up again and then slammed it down. "Just how do you expect to get all the way out here?"

"Ever heard of a bus?" she shouted.

His brows crashed low over his eyes. "There is no bus for three miles."

She scraped her chair back. "Then I'll walk!"

Shira made it to the front door before the tears fell, and she slammed the door in her wake. While she stomped across the front lawn, she cursed herself for being an idiot. She'd let him see as plain as day how she felt about him, and that was the last thing she wanted.

"Shira," Whisper called out behind her.

Shira stopped walking and scrubbed her face. She sniffed and turned with what she hoped was an apologetic smile. "I'm sorry. I didn't mean to get in the way of you and your boyfriend. I know you don't know me that well, but I promise I won't steal anything at your apartment. You don't have to stay there and entertain me."

"How about we catch a movie tonight?" Whisper said.

Her offer took Shira by surprise. "I…uh…"

Whisper linked her arm through Shira's and turned her so they could continue walking away from the house. "You need a break. I know what a stubborn ass Max can be. Trust me. I love him like a brother, but whew, a handful. Anyway, don't worry about Alec and me. We're good. After what you told me though, I think you need a girl's night out. We could do dinner and a movie. Or we could go to a club."

"Ah, dinner and a movie would be great," Shira admitted. "It's been a long time since I've been to a theater. I don't know what's playing."

"Leave that to me." Whisper patted her arm. "Leave Max to me too."

* * * *

Max stood by the window overlooking the front lawn. He watched the two women talking and wondered what Shira was telling Whisper about him. He'd seen her wipe her face and knew she was crying. He hated making her cry, but it was better that she realize there could be nothing between them. He'd be crueler letting her believe something that would never happen.

"So, you said there's nothing going on between you," his brother said, still at the table eating. Of course he was happy and content. Max knew the argument between him and Whisper meant nothing. They were sealed as one.

"Do I need to repeat myself?" he grumbled. Whisper was right. His attitude hadn't improved. He glanced over his shoulder to find his brother buttering toast. The calm irritated him.

"That's funny," Alec said, not looking up, "because I smell *you* all over her."

"Shut up!"

Alec laughed. "Oh, so I hit a nerve. Tell me you haven't had sex with her, brother."

"I don't have to deny that." He swung from the window and returned to the table. His eggs were cold, so he poured himself another cup of coffee. "I fucked her."

"Careful," Alec warned.

Max sighed. He didn't want to disrespect Shira even to prove to his brother she didn't mean anything. "We had sex. It meant nothing."

"She can be your mate. I think it's obvious to one and all that she cares about you."

Max clenched the cup's handle so tight, he thought it might snap at any moment. He willed himself to relax. "She's human."

"So?"

"So she's not my mate. I had a mate. She died."

"Max."

He slammed the cup down, sloshing liquid over the sides onto the tablecloth. He recalled Shira had placed it on the table fresh the day before. She'd have his head for the stain. *Damn it, that doesn't matter. She's leaving.*

"She's not my mate," he insisted. "You know as well as I do we mate for life. When Sarah died, that was it for me."

"It doesn't have to be." Alec narrowed his eyes on Max. "Unless of course she's not the sweet thing she appears to be."

Max grunted. "She is. Shira needs...well, she needs someone to look after her."

His brother's eyebrow rose. "If you know that, then you know you can be that one. Max, if you don't get your head out of your ass, you're going to miss what's right in front of you."

"I don't want her. Not now. Not ever."

Alec didn't answer. When Max raised his attention from the mess he was trying to get up, he noticed Alec staring past him. Dread tightened the muscles of his stomach, and he turned around. Whisper and Shira were standing in the doorway. There was no doubt in his mind that Shira had heard his last words and knew they were about her. He was the worst of all men and the biggest fool.

"Shira—"

She held up a hand and directed such a scathing look at him, he flinched. "Don't even. Whisper, want to keep me company cleaning up this mess? Then we can get out of here."

Whisper's gaze raked over him as if he was nothing more than scum. That hurt. He loved her like a sister. Then she nodded to Shira. "Yeah, sure."

Shira walked over to the table and took up his plate without asking if he was done. She nabbed his coffee cup and his silverware and disappeared into the kitchen. He knew he should say something to her, but maybe this was for the best. She would get along a lot better if she was angry and not hurt. He'd handled everything wrong, but none of them seemed to understand that he could not have a second mate. To even try was an insult to Sarah's memory. He scraped his chair back and stood up. What he needed right now was a run—*bad*. He met his brother's gaze and saw agreement there. Alec would join in their leopard forms and run off some steam through the woods. Maybe when he was done, Shira's face wouldn't loom in his mind's eye bringing with it guilt and an odd tightness in his chest.

Chapter Eight

Shira laughed at every funny scene in the movie and traded comments with Whisper as they watched. On some level she enjoyed herself, and her smile never wavered, but deep inside, a weight pressed on her. She couldn't stop thinking of Max and of what he'd said. Whisper had lit into him. Shira had heard them arguing while she kicked herself for cowering in the kitchen. The truth of the matter was she was angry, but if she said one word to Max, she thought she might break down. She'd given enough of her tears to Sam, and he didn't deserve them. Max wasn't getting any. Not after what he'd said.

She kept leaning toward making excuses for him, telling herself that he was just hurt from losing the woman he loved. She wanted to tell herself that he was cut off from his emotions, but whether that was true or not, she couldn't afford to give in to thoughts like that. They were what led to her staying in a relationship that was not good for her. Never again.

"Hey." Whisper tapped her arm. "Movie over. Where are you?"

Shira blushed. "Oh, sorry. My mind was wandering." She forced another smile.

"Stop!"

Shira jumped at the sharpness in Whisper's tone.

"You're pretending to be on top of the world, and you don't have to. I know what it's like to be hurt when you give yourself to someone and they throw your gift back at you."

Shira stilled at Whisper's words. She didn't want to hear it, but her friend went on.

"I could have ripped Max a new one for the way he acted and what he said. I know he's not that kind of man, but there he was acting like it, and that I won't stand for." She rose, and Shira did as well. She couldn't bring herself to say a word, but then Whisper didn't seem to need a response. "I think he cares about you. He just doesn't know how to face it. He thinks he's betraying Sarah."

This time Shira did comment. "Don't. I can't hear that right now. I get it that he likes me. He may even want me again after… Well, whatever. I'm over it. I admit I feel a little sad, but we've only known each other a short while. No need to throw myself into a depression because he said some mean words. Please, I've heard that and much worse."

Whisper took her hand and held it. "I'm so sorry. You're the last person to deserve him acting like that."

Shira shrugged it off as if it was nothing, which was so not true. "My past made me stronger. Come on. I'm hungry. Let's get dinner."

They left the theater and walked down the street in the direction of the stores and restaurants. Shira noticed Whisper power up her cell phone. She needed one if she was going to get calls for jobs. She tallied the money she had and didn't think she could afford anything other than a pay as you go phone for the time being.

Whisper made a noise of frustration, capturing Shira's attention. Her friend handed over the phone, and Shira read the text message. *"Whisper, please have Shira give me a call. I need to talk to her."*

Shira handed the phone back just as it rang.

"Speak of the devil," Whisper said. "You want to talk to him?"

"Nope."

Whisper chuckled and pressed a button that made the phone stop ringing. "So where are we eating?"

They found a restaurant and sat down. Soon they had drinks at their elbows and menus in hand. Shira automatically scanned the prices more so than the food itself.

"Get whatever you want," Whisper said. "My treat."

"You got the movie. I can get this," she said.

"You can get everything the next time," Whisper insisted.

Pride made Shira want to argue, but she had to give in. One way or another, she would get on firm ground. "Okay, fine. And thanks."

"You got it. We have to stick together."

Shira was half way through her dinner, at last able to fully enjoy herself, when she glanced up and froze in place. On the other side of the restaurant sat Sam with a woman.

"You look pale, Shira. Are you okay?" Whisper asked.

She opened her mouth to speak, but the words were nothing more than a breath. "Fine."

"Who's that?" Whisper said, obviously following her line of sight.

"My ex."

"That's him? The asshole that—"

"Yeah."

Her friend sucked her teeth. "I think I should get Alec to kick his ass."

"Whisper!"

"What? He deserves it."

Shira snapped out of her shock and fear, and laughed. "Yeah, he does. Thanks for the sentiment, but no, leave him alone. As long as he stays out of my life, I'm happy staying out of his."

"And you should be."

Shira made herself finish her meal even while her appetite had taken a nosedive. She would not let Sam steal anything else from her, including the delicious steak, baked potato, and side salad she had ordered. She had just swallowed the last bite and was wiping her mouth when a shadow blocked the light on her right. She looked up into Sam's blue eyes.

"Shira, I thought that was you," he almost simpered. "How are you?"

She stiffened when he leaned down and kissed her cheek. Whisper moved as if to stand, but Shira put her hand out. The anger rolling off her friend must have been obvious to Sam, but he acted like he didn't notice. Shira glanced at Sam's companion and caught an expression of resentment and jealousy, but she focused on Sam. Not paying him attention had cost her, and it was habit to do so now.

"Sam," she said. There was no need to get into a conversation with him. The sooner he moved on, the better. She wasn't going for the acting like they were old friends even if she was scared of him. A sense of panic had risen in her when his lips touched her cheek, but he hadn't pushed it by staying close.

"I've missed you, Shira," Sam went on. She chewed the inside of her cheek, hating him. Sam kept his distance, and his tone of voice was low and pleasant. Yet, he provoked emotions in her that she couldn't explain. "Looks like you've put on a little weight."

You always hated me so thin. Their short time apart hardly made that much of a difference, but then eating regularly without drama didn't take a lot to gain.

Shira clutched her hands in her lap and drew courage from somewhere deep. "Save your comments or compliments—or whatever they're supposed to be—for someone who doesn't know you like I do." She eyed the woman and then focused back on him. "You're not real, and what's more important, I don't give a damn what you think."

The rage that flashed in his eyes made her want to run, but she stood her ground. He sucked in a deep breath and then smiled. "You hurt me, honey."

"Don't call her honey, fucker," Whisper snapped. "Why don't you just go about your business. Your girlfriend is getting jealous."

Whisper's words seemed to be too much for him. He whirled on her. "Know your place, before I put you in it."

Her friend stood up, hands on her hips. "Oh please try. *Pretty please!* My boyfriend would put you in the ground without breaking a sweat." She looked Sam up and down. "Matter of fact, I'm sure I can take you myself, a spoiled little egghead like you."

Shira sat there in awe. She didn't know if she should laugh or drag Whisper back into her seat. She'd run her mouth too many times to Sam, and she never felt like he'd completely broken her. Still, even *she* wouldn't have gone so far as to belittle him to his face. Whisper was brave, but then she could afford to be with a man like Alec behind her. What she'd said was probably true. Shira had seen the way Alec looked at Whisper. She bet he wouldn't think twice about killing Sam because he put his hands on Whisper.

Sam's face turned beet red. His nostrils flared, and he flexed his fingers at his sides. Even his date seemed surprised at his attitude and the way he appeared to be seconds from attacking Whisper. Shira reached out and pulled her friend's hand.

"Don't let him provoke you. He's not worth it," she said.

"Listen to your friend," Sam pushed between clenched teeth.

They faced off for long minutes, but Sam was the one to turn away first. Whisper hadn't blinked, nor had she backed down. Shira found herself wondering if Whisper would be that brave if she had no one to protect her and if she'd already suffered blow after blow from this man. Maybe some people were different. Maybe Whisper would have beaten him in his sleep and walked out. She admired her friend's grit no matter what.

Sam uttered something insulting and turned to walk away. Then he came back and leaned close to Shira's ear. "You remember what I told you, don't you, honey?"

She stifled a tremor but said nothing. Sam left the restaurant at a clipped pace. His date had to almost run to keep up with him, and he didn't hold the door for her as he disappeared through the exit.

"You had to deal with that for how many years?" Whisper asked.

Shira shook herself. "Five years. I was stupid, but I'm over it now."

Whisper studied her. "Not yet, but I'm here for you, sweetie. Everything is going to be fine. I promise."

Shira nodded, but she was beginning to wonder. Discussing the situation would do no good, so she changed the subject. For the rest of the evening, Sam occupied her thoughts and what to do about him.

* * * *

Shira snapped her earring into place and peered at herself in the mirror. She'd changed them three times from the selection Whisper had given her. The dress she wore was figure-hugging and short. The smooth, silky material stopped halfway up her thighs, and the neckline plunged a little lower than she wanted, but Whisper had convinced her to buy it along with a pair of sling backs that made her legs look longer than they were. Not that she didn't think she looked good. She had to admit she did. The problem was, she wasn't happy about going to this party tonight. Max was escorting her, and from what she could gather, his brother had coerced him into doing it for the sake of their business.

"Oh, wow," Whisper exclaimed when she stepped into the room, "you look amazing. Max is going to be drooling over you all night."

Shira rolled her eyes. "Please. The only reason he's taking me is because of his business or whatever he and Alec are up to."

Whisper walked over and began working a curl Shira had let fall at her temple while she'd put up the rest of her hair. She'd been to plenty of fancy functions on Sam's arm, so she was an old hand at putting herself together.

"They're trying to convince some mogul or whatever to get up off this commercial property they want," Whisper explained. "He's throwing this party, and they figure they'll charm him. Alec is pretty good at that kind of thing."

Shira wondered if Max was when he tried. The last week of him picking her up from Whisper's apartment and taking her home in the evening wasn't the best experience. He was quiet most of the time and gruff when he spoke. He mostly left her notes with instructions while he disappeared somewhere, but then later he would insist they have their meals together. He pissed her off, but this was their relationship until she found something else. Now that she was building a good friendship with Whisper, she couldn't make herself leave town, even if Sam wasn't far away. What to do about him still plagued her. She could only hope he would lose interest and move on.

"Well, why do I have to go?"

Whisper smacked her on the shoulder. "Because I'm not going to be bored mindless with those two talking business all night. Besides, you need to get out, so you're going."

Shira laughed. Whisper did push her more to live, and she didn't mind. If she had her way, her face would be to the grindstone working overtime at some job so she could save. That dinner and movie the other night had been great aside from the run-in with Sam. She needed to unwind sometimes. "Fine. I'm ready. You look awesome by the way."

Whisper did a spin. Her dress extended just a bit longer than Shira's, but it was no less sexy. The style and vibrant color played up Whisper's generous figure and set off her big breasts. Shira looked down at her own and sighed. *Oh well, it is what it is.*

They left the bedroom just as the doorbell rang. Shira drew back, sudden nerves stirring in her belly, but her friend had no such reservations. Shira had noticed Whisper seemed lonely when she wasn't with Alec, and they called or texted constantly when they were apart. She'd never seen two people more in love.

When Whisper threw open the door, she launched herself into Alec's arms, and he whipped her around as if she weighed nothing. "You didn't even look through the peephole," he complained. "It could have been a dangerous stranger."

"I knew it was you," Whisper assured him, and they were lost in a kiss so hungry Whisper would have to redo her lipstick when it was over.

With a sigh of impatience, Max stepped around his brother and Whisper into the apartment. Shira smoothed her moist palms over her dress. "Hey," she said.

He stared. His expression was so blank, she couldn't tell if he thought she looked a mess or he liked what he saw. "Well?" she demanded to cover her nerves.

His gaze swept her from head to foot. "You look fine. Isn't that a bit too much skin showing?"

She swung away about to return to the bedroom when he was all of a sudden behind her, grabbing for her hand to keep her where she was. He stood too close, which meant he had to hear her racing heart. Damn him.

"You don't have a bra on," he said softly.

That was obvious because the back of her dress was cut low. One couldn't wear a bra with it. "Is that all you can do? Complain? If you don't like it, you don't have to be seen with me."

His warm breath stirred the loose tendrils at her nape. "Let me make this plain. The only reason I haven't already ripped that dress off of your hot, little body is because I have business to take care of. But you knew the impact dressing like this would have on me, didn't you? Let's go."

Shira blushed. Max's compliment was rough, even angrily given, but the impact was way more powerful than if he'd just said, "You look nice." She couldn't help being pleased with it. *Yeah, he has the charm ability all right.*

The party was being held at the mansion of the man Alec and Max wanted to do business with. As soon as she and Max pulled up in his car, Shira lost her breath. The fact that it was nighttime did not hide the beauty of the place. Outside lighting flooded the circular driveway, and when they stopped, a valet moved forward to park the car. Shira tightened her hold on Max's hand as he helped her from the car.

"Am I dressed right for something like this?" she worried.

He smiled, and she was lost. "You look perfect. Will you fish for compliments all night?"

She rolled her eyes at him, but his dig had done the trick. Her nerves fluttered away, and she was able to walk into the house without too much care.

All around them were other guests dressed to the nines and looking like they were born with money. To her surprise, Max stayed close while she and Whisper were introduced to their host.

"Alec, Max," a thin, balding man in a dark suit called out. "Good to see you, and who are these two beauties?"

Alec put Whisper forward. "Corbin, this is my fiancée, Whisper Price. Whisper, this is Corbin Mancini."

Corbin shook Whisper's hand with a friendly smile, but he turned right away to Shira. "And you are?"

Max spoke before she could. "This is Shira Hill, her friend."

Embarrassment crept up Shira's back. He'd put her with Whisper even though he stood at her side. Pissed off, she stepped away from him toward Corbin and held out her hand. "How are you?"

He took her hand and tugged her a little closer than necessary. "Very well *now*. So this one didn't claim you for himself?"

"Claim?" Whisper blurted as if it was some kind of key term. Alec shook his head, and Shira wondered what the big deal was.

"You can be my special guest tonight, my lovely lady," Corbin told her and tucked her hand on his arm to lead her farther into the house. He called over his shoulder, "Alec, Max, Whisper, enjoy the party."

Shira was tempted to look back at Max, but she straightened her shoulders and raised her head. Why should she cling to him when he didn't want her? This man thought she was beautiful, and even if he didn't do it for her, hell, he could be fun for the time being.

Face after face zipped by her as Corbin introduced her. Shira had learned the art of conversation in a way that kept most of the attention on the person talking to her or the man at her side. Sam had drilled the skill home, so she had no trouble keeping anyone from knowing she was a housekeeper and a college dropout.

Dancing started up in a room set aside for it, and Shira was surprised to find she didn't lack partners. She scanned the room for Whisper and located her at the side of the room looking slightly bored and holding a glass of wine. Alec and Max stood a few feet away speaking with several other men. A man approached Whisper looking too eager. He said something to Whisper, and she smiled but shook her head. Shira almost laughed when she pointed out Alec and the guy took in Alec's heated glare. He backpedaled and almost fell over his feet to escape. Shira sighed. No one would care about her that much.

The song ended, and she extricated herself from her dance partner. She couldn't remember his name. "If you'll excuse me, I'm going to take a break. Thank you for the dance," she said.

The man, who extended only to her shoulder, held onto her hand. "Can I find you later?"

"Um…"

"Shira."

She jumped at the voice because it was so unexpected. Her mouth went dry, and she spun slowly to her left. Sam approached her. This was too much of a coincidence. This city wasn't so small that they had to rub shoulders at every opportunity. "Sam, what are you—?"

"Doing here?" He grinned, and a raised eyebrow sent her dance partner on his way. Right then, she'd be happier with the squat man than Sam. "Did you forget how many people I know, Shira? Maybe you forgot what I told you."

She gritted her teeth.

He took her hand just as another song started up. She was about to snatch it away, when he spoke again. "Corbin Mancini is a good friend of mine. Imagine the conversation he and I held regarding Max Macgregor."

She froze. "You don't… You couldn't have…"

He led her into a slow dance, a palm at her lower back while he clutched her hand in a grip she couldn't escape. "Did you think I would walk away so easily? I told you if you wanted to defy me, I would ruin that bastard's life. I have already begun. If he thinks he's making a deal with Corbin, he will be sorely mistaken."

"Sam, don't do this," she begged. "Max has nothing to do with me. I work for him. That's all, and when I find something else, I won't see him. He doesn't even like me."

He scowled, his face crumbling so much that it made him ugly and shook her to her core in its evil. "Yet I see desperation to save him in your eyes. If I thought that you loved him—no, that's impossible. Did you fuck him, Shira?"

Her fingers spasmed under his. "None of your damn business."

"Which is a yes." He squeezed her hand until she gasped. She would not give him the satisfaction of crying out. Never again.

"Let go of me."

His response was to draw her closer until their bodies touched. Memories of their nights in bed together flooded her mind and made her sick. She wished she could block out the past and never think of it again.

"You still want to fight me?" He tsked. "Where is this coming from? Him? Did opening your legs for him make you bold, Shira? Tell me, did he say he loves you, that he'll protect you from me?"

She looked away. Of course Max had never said that. Hell, he'd denied even bringing her as his date tonight. He wouldn't protect her. She had only herself to depend on, and yet, she couldn't let Sam punish Max because of her. Tears filled her eyes, and she did everything she could to blink them away. Whatever hope she'd been feeling about her life fizzled. How had she thought she could stay in town? Whisper's friendship had made her think she could stick around, and on some level, she had resolved to enjoy seeing Max's face even if she couldn't be with him.

Sam's threats weren't empty. Although he was a doctor, she had seen him destroy men before. Not because of her, but because they had crossed him in some way. He had influence in ways she could only imagine until she'd seen them first hand. His family came from money, too, and his father had political ties. Sam had never backed down from using every resource available to him to get to people. Max might not be the poor man she had first assumed him to be, but he was still just a real estate businessman. He couldn't hope to match Sam's influence. She had to do what she could to protect him, especially since it was her fault that Sam had turned his evil in Max's direction.

"I'm not going back to his house," she offered in a low tone of resignation. "I'll tell him I quit and never see him again."

"Of course you will." The confidence in Sam's voice grated on her, but she didn't say a word. He continued laying down the directives. "You will move out of that girl's apartment and come to me tonight."

She started at his words and looked up at him. He chuckled.

"Did you think I didn't know where you were? I let you get comfortable, give yourself enough rope until I was ready to jerk you back where you belong."

"I have to go to the restroom." If she didn't get out of there now, she was going to cry in front of everyone, and that would be worse. Sam would be embarrassed and make her life even more of a living hell. "Please, I have to go."

He turned her, and as calm as if they were taking an evening stroll, walked her toward the room's exit. When they drew up to it, Max stepped in front of them. He stood with easy confidence, one hand tucked into his pocket. A smile graced his sexy full lips, but she picked up on the anger in his eyes and the tension in his shoulders. "You've been busy all night, Shira. I think this is my dance."

She opened her mouth to speak, but Sam cut her off. "You're mistaken. My fiancée dances only with me."

Max's nostrils flared. "Since when is she your fiancée? My

understanding is she dumped your sorry ass. Couldn't get it up or something like that. She hasn't had any complaints since she came to live with me."

Shira gasped, and Sam went red. His fingers dug into her lower back. That's all she needed was for Max to confirm that they'd been lovers. Even if it was only once, that was one time too many for Sam.

"Tell him you've agreed to be my wife, Shira," Sam said.

Max's gaze slid from Sam's face to hers. She could read him with no problem right now. His expression said all she had to do was say the word and he'd wipe the floor with Sam. She suspected that was only an excuse because he didn't like Sam, not because he cared about her.

She drew in a deep breath and raised her chin. Hey, if they could act, so could she. "He's right. Back off, Max. Sam and I are getting married. I don't need you anymore. I won't be coming back to work. Thanks for everything."

Her mask was about to crumble, so she ducked around Max and beat a hasty retreat out the door. The bathroom was too busy with women, so she found the nearest exit and jetted outside. Cool air eased the heat in her face but did nothing to calm her emotions. The tears fell.

She ran along the drive, but when she heard laughter from other guests who had wandered outside, she left the paved drive and hurried into the trees. The mansion must lie on several acres, and she was glad of it. She could disappear until she pulled herself together.

She found a tree to lean on and sobbed her eyes out. Seeing Max again was impossible, but returning to Sam's wasn't an option. She couldn't go back into that nightmare now that she had tasted freedom. *I won't go back. I can't!*

Chapter Nine

Shira took a step in the direction of the street. If she could make it to the main road, she could flag down a taxi and get to Whisper's apartment to pack. Then she would catch a bus out of town. With any luck, Sam would think she was in the bathroom, or maybe he and Max were still arguing. She heaved a sigh remembering the many times she had run before.

"Shira."

She stopped and turned. The moon had passed behind clouds, so there wasn't much light. She just made him out standing in the trees.

"Where are you going?"

"What do you care?" she demanded.

He strode closer just as the moon reappeared, and her heartbeat picked up seeing his handsome face. Why did she have to long for him when he didn't give a crap about her?

Max stopped in front of her and ran a finger down her cheek. She turned away, but he made her look at him. His touch burned, making her desire him like no other man. He had to know what he did to her.

"I-I have to go," she whispered.

"Where?"

She was so lost and so scared, she closed her eyes willing everything to go away, including Max. He didn't budge but wrapped his arm around her waist. A sob escaped her, and she struggled to hold it in.

"Don't," she pleaded.

He kissed her lips, and she clung to him. His tongue found its way into her mouth, teasing her with his flavor and making her crazy with need. Shira pulled away and pushed at his chest. He didn't let go, but his hold loosened.

"This is not what you want," he told her.

"How do you know?" She turned her back on him and walked a couple of paces. Everything inside of her wanted him to stop her and for him to tell her she couldn't leave him. Max wasn't the type to throw himself at her and make wild declarations of love, but here she was hoping for it. *Girl, seriously, wake up to reality.*

"If you choose to quit working for me, that's fine," he said. "We don't ever have to have sex again."

Her heart clenched in pain.

"But you're a fool if you marry him."

Shira didn't think twice. She whirled on him and smacked his face as hard as she could. "And you're an asshole!"

She took off running through the trees, swiping at branches that clawed at her face and hair. Several times, she tripped, and once she fell. She scrambled to her feet and ran some more. She had no idea of the direction she took, whether she headed to the road or back toward the house. All she knew was that she had to keep moving.

When she came to a wooden fence that blocked her path, she stopped. The scratches on her arms burned, and she was so upset that she didn't care if the one on her face left a scar. Her chest hurt from running, and a stitch had started in her side. She panted, trying to recover. A sound in the darkness to her right had her calming heart rate kicking up. She stiffened, and then from the shadows came the leopard.

"It's you," she exclaimed. "How did you find me out here?"

She was still nervous around the animal, but with the mess of the humans in her life, the leopard seemed like a welcome relief. She dropped to her knees feeling the cool earth under them and knowing she probably looked a hot mess. The leopard came to her with gentle grace. She wrapped her arms around him and laid her face in his fur.

The sobs she'd held in check came unbidden, and she let the tears fall for a long time.

After some time, she raised her head sniffling. She scratched the cat behind his ears, and he purred. "I'm not going back," she said. "To either of them."

The leopard pulled from her hold and turned away from her.

"You're leaving me too?"

The way it bobbed its head she could have sworn it told her no, but she decided she was seeing things. The leopard paced toward the trees away from the fence and then stopped. She figured out that it wanted her to follow. She stood up and went after him. They walked for what felt like hours. She dug the cheap cell phone she had purchased out of her purse and saw that it had been forty-five minutes. Missed calls reminded her that she had put her cell phone on vibrate earlier and hadn't taken it off. Whisper had phoned three times, but Max hadn't. She sighed. He didn't give a damn, so why should she?

The leopard led her out to the road, and she couldn't believe he was smart enough to have done that. She stooped and kissed his head. "Thanks, sweetie."

She started to walk along the street, but the leopard crossed in front of her, blocking her path. She stopped. Behind her, she heard a car coming, and she shrank back to the tree line in fear. She considered running the way she had come, but again the leopard blocked her. Lights blinded her when the car pulled to a stop. Her heart raced.

"Shira," a man called. At first she thought it was Max, but then she realized it was his brother Alec. "Come on. Get in."

She wondered why he didn't say anything about the leopard, but maybe he couldn't see it in the shadows. She waited to see if the animal would stop her again, but he didn't. Exhausted, she had no choice but to take the ride. Maybe Alec could run her to the apartment and then take her to the bus station.

Alec got out of the car and walked around to open the passenger door. She sighed and got in. He shut the door and then opened the back one. Shira's eyes widened when he held it until the leopard got in, and then he hopped in on his side. Her throat was dry as they rode down the street.

"You know him?" she asked after some time.

"Yeah."

She waited for an explanation, but he didn't offer one. "Um, I was wondering if you could take me to Whisper's apartment to pick up my things and then take me to the bus station."

The leopard growled in the back, and Alec gave him a look that appeared to be a warning. The animal fell silent.

"Is that what you really want?" Alec asked.

She frowned. "Does it matter?"

"I heard... I mean my brother mentioned to me that you were planning to marry your ex. My understanding was that relationship wasn't the best."

"Wow, word travels fast." She waved her hand. "Well, you all can relax. I'm not marrying Sam, but neither am I going to keep working for Max. I'm leaving."

"Whisper won't be happy. It seemed like the two of your were getting close."

She clutched her purse so tight her fingers hurt. "Why is everyone so quick to tell me what *they* want?"

He stared at her a second. "I wasn't aware that was happening." Alec pulled to the side of the road and came to a stop. He jumped out of the car, and she watched him march around to her side and open the door. *Oh goodness, he's so mad he's going to leave me on the side of the road.*

"I sorry," she blurted. "I didn't mean..."

He tugged her from the car and slammed the door before the leopard could get out. "Walk with me a little."

Shira pressed her lips together. Both brothers were bossy. She gave in and fell into step beside him. They paced a short way from the car, and she looked back to see that the leopard was not pleased to be trapped in Alec's vehicle.

"My brother likes you. *A lot*," Alec began.

"I don't think so." She fidgeted with her dress, embarrassed.

"He's been hurt. The pain of his loss goes deeper than anything you could imagine. I'm only now getting it. If I imagine losing Whisper, I can see the despair he must have felt."

"Why are you telling me this?" She shrugged as if it didn't matter. "I said I'm leaving, so I don't have any false hopes in his direction."

"That's the wrong move."

She put her hands on her hips. "Excuse me?"

He grumbled, giving a good impression of the gruff noises the leopard had made earlier. "My brother is a fool, but it's clear to me if you leave, you're doing the same thing Sarah did."

Shira blinked up at him. "What?"

"Sarah left him. It might not have been her fault, but she left him alone. You're doing the same."

"In case you didn't know, your brother pushed me away. You heard him yourself say he doesn't want me. Besides, we were only employer and employee, nothing more."

"Don't lie to yourself."

She stomped her foot and started to walk back to the car. "Please take me home. I'll find my own way to the bus station. And if you don't want to do that, then I'll walk!"

"Two stubborn asses," he muttered.

She whirled around. "What did you say?"

"Nothing," he snapped. "Get in."

A short while later, they drew up to the apartment building. Shira hesitated in getting out. "What will you do with him?" She indicated the leopard.

"I'll take care of him. Don't worry. And I'll tell Whisper you're okay."

She thanked him and got out. Now that she was home, she realized she was too tired to pack let alone get to the station. There wasn't a doubt in her mind Sam would come by at some point, so she would set her alarm to wake her at five in the morning, then get moving.

After a hot shower, she slipped into a nightie, ready to go to bed. The doorbell ringing stopped her in her tracks, and fear kept her where she was. Had Sam come straight over? He'd said he had known all along where she was staying. Whisper had said earlier that she was spending the night with Alec. She was alone.

Shira searched the apartment for a weapon. If she knew Sam, he wouldn't go away until she answered. He would stand out there knocking until she worried he would disturb the neighbors.

Whisper had placed a bat in the hall closet, and Shira retrieved it, gripping the handle as she approached the door.

"Go away, Sam. I'm not coming back." She couldn't make herself get close enough to the door to check the peephole.

"Shira, it's me."

Her heart fluttered. "Max?"

She threw the locks back and wrenched the door open. There he was, looking oddly like he'd been desperate to see her. She decided she was fantasizing from all the stress of the evening.

Max eyed the bat still in her hand. "Were you planning to bludgeon me to death?"

She let the weapon drop to her side. "What do you want?"

"Don't go."

"What?" She didn't just hear the words she'd longed for him to say. Her imagination had run into overtime.

Max stepped into the apartment, forcing her to retreat a pace. He shut the door and locked it, then turned back to her. From the first touch of his hands on her upper arms, she was lost, but she forced herself to remain silent.

"I don't want you to go," he said. "Stay here with me."

She lowered her gaze to his shirtfront. He hadn't changed, but his suit jacket was gone, and his shirt had wrinkles that weren't there earlier. "I'm sure you can find another housekeeper."

Okay, so she was pushing it, but the man wasn't spouting words of love. The least he could do was be plain about what he wanted. All she knew was that her heart had gone haywire, and it was taking a lot of willpower not to bury her face at the base of his neck and plead for him not to let go. She had more pride than that.

Max cupped her face between his palms and made her look him in the eyes. The intensity in his gaze took her breath away. She had to part her lips and draw in air just to keep from falling to the floor. *He's a rebound relationship. Not more than that. I can't afford to love him so deeply.*

"Please... Shira..."

Blood pulsed in her ears making it hard to hear, but she read his lips. They were so close. He didn't speak words of love, but she saw the longing and what she hadn't expected to see, although it echoed in her own heart.

"I can't be alone," he said. "Not again. I don't know what's right or what's wrong. I can't let you go. Stay."

She nodded, swallowing before she could say anything. "I won't leave you."

Her feet left the floor when he scooped her into a crushing embrace. He didn't hurt her, but he devoured her lips and moaned in her mouth like she was a lifeline. He kissed her long and hard, until she felt lightheaded. Her body ignited, and she wrapped her legs around his waist. He carried her down the hall as he continued to drop soft caresses to her cheeks, her eyes, her temples.

He loves me. He must *love me.*

He laid her on the bed and rested a big palm on her mound. Shira trembled. Her nightie had risen, revealing her panties. The flimsy pink thing was a barrier she needed gone now. She reached down to slide them over her hips, but he stopped her.

TWIN LEOPARDS — Tressie Lockwood

"Wait."

She paused, eying him. "Don't you want to?"

"Woman, are you mad?" He chuckled. "Let me look at you for a minute. Let me feast on your slender curves, the soft, chocolate skin, so smooth and tastes so good." He demonstrated his meaning by leaning down and brushing her nightie higher to reveal her belly. A gentle kiss there sent shivers down her spine. He helped her get the nightie over her head and stopped to stare once again.

"You don't think I'm too thin?" Getting his ex's well-endowed figure out of her head was difficult. To fill a B cup bra was a challenge for her, and when she'd lost so much weight being with Sam, she'd gone down to an A. She had never heard the end of it.

Max flicked a thumb over one of her nipples and licked his lips. She didn't miss the lust in his eyes. "Your breasts fit in my hand perfectly, and I don't think I've met a woman with such large nipples. Is that normal for black women?"

He seemed genuinely curious, and Shira rolled her eyes. "Are you going to try to find out?"

He lowered his head and kissed her pussy through her panties. Shira caught her bottom lip between her teeth and raised her hips a little. Max drew away to her disappointment. "Do you want to be the only black woman I ever have? The only woman *period?*"

She gasped. Was he asking he to marry him? He couldn't be. Not like this.

Max didn't seem to expect an answer. He at last removed her panties, the whole of his attention focused between her legs. All of Shira's doubts about her body melted away, and she raised a knee and spread her thighs. She knew he liked what he saw. She could please him and bring him to a strong release if nothing else. Knowing whether he loved her was a mystery, but for now, this was enough. This pleasure between the two of them, however long it lasted.

She played with her nipples for him, twisting the peaks and

massaging them while she moaned. A low growl started in Max's throat, and he went still watching her. She squeezed her breasts and arched her back, then ran her hands down her belly. At her mound, she used one hand to play with her pussy. She parted her folds and fingered her clit. All the while a light danced in his eyes. Shira could have sworn they changed color, but she wasn't sure.

Max licked his lips once again. "Put your finger inside. Let me see it covered in your come."

She did as she was told, not minding the command at all. "Like this?"

"Yes, just like that." If possible, his voice had gone deeper if a bit craggy. She liked it. "Now two fingers, baby. Oh, yeah, deeper."

She ran her fingers in and out of her pussy, getting off on the sounds her cream made. She raised her hips and gasped her pleasure. "I wish it was you in me."

"What part of me?"

She turned her head away. He tsked, and turned her head back before focusing on her pussy again.

"Tell me what part of my body you want down here, Shira."

Nervous and a little embarrassed, she didn't say anything. Max leaned down and kissed her lips. She ached to be filled, but dirty talk wasn't something she'd done before. The mere thought got her hotter, but saying it out loud. Using the *P* word seemed too clinical and was a turnoff.

She shut her eyes tight and blurted, "Your dick."

She expected his laugh, but his lips touched hers a brief second and then were gone. "Can you say cock?"

"Cock." She threw her arm over her face. "You must think I'm an idiot. I promise I'm not so virginal."

This time he did chuckle. "I have first hand knowledge that you're not. Open your eyes for me, Shira. I want us to look at each other when we come."

She peered up at him, and the embarrassment ebbed.

"Does it bother you to say it?"

She shook her head. "It turns me on. I want you to talk dirty to me, Max."

"In that case…" He sat up and began dragging his clothes off and tossing them over his shoulder. "The sooner I get my hard cock inside your tight, little pussy, the better. I'm about to explode, and I want to do it buried as deep as I can get. Now"—he positioned himself over her—"would you like me to fuck you in the ass as well?"

Shira's pussy gushed anew. "Hell, yes!"

Max stroked a hand over her mound and squeezed. "So wet, baby. You're all ready for me, aren't you?"

She raised her legs higher, causing her pussy lips to open more. "I need it now, Max."

"Mm, do you know what you do to me?" He ran a hand from the base of his cock to the tip, and her mouth watered just seeing how stiff he was. She knew even though they'd had sex for hours the last time, it had been too long. He would stretch her, and she'd welcome it.

Max caressed her cheek and leaned down over her. The tip of his cock touched her entrance. She moaned, and when her lids lowered, he tapped her cheek. Shira focused on him. She tried to hide it, but something told her all the love she felt for him was plain in her face. An expression of surprise came over him, but then he smiled. He pushed into her, and she cried out his name.

"Take it all, baby," he whispered. "Every inch belongs to you now. I won't be with another woman, Shira. Only you."

Tears filled her eyes. She shook all over and wrapped her arms around his shoulders. His skin was hot and moist. His muscles contracted with each thrust, and she couldn't get enough. Not of touching him or of feeling him invade her body. He claimed her in the basest of ways, and she offered herself up to him. When her orgasm came, she screamed and threw her head back. Max captured her chin, forcing her to face him. She'd always closed her eyes, so it was hard to focus on him. Something told her he needed it. He needed *her*, and knowing that was scary and exciting all at the same time. *He needs* me.

"Max."

"Shira." He thrust harder and faster. His breath came in short, harsh bursts. When he tensed in his jaw, she knew he was ready to come. He let go, but his gaze never wavered from hers. She melted into him as if his soul opened up and took her in. A sense of wildness came over her, and for a moment, terror welled, but Max's gentle voice cut through. They were together, and it was okay. He was stronger than any man she'd ever met, and vulnerable too. Max hadn't wanted to let go of his pain because facing a future alone was more than he thought he could bear. She didn't know everything about him, but she knew that. She would do whatever it took to help him heal, and maybe one day he would come to love her as she loved him.

Chapter Ten

Max had to admit he felt better having accepted his desire for Shira. She meant a lot to him. He knew that. Pushing her away had been hard. He'd thought it was for the best and found out real quick, it wouldn't work. He needed her. So, he could admit that too. Now that she had decided to stay, he had greater peace, even happiness. They had spent the entire night in bed together, and then he had insisted they transfer her stuff to his house. He had no intention of letting her move out again. In fact, he had brought her clothes to his bedroom where they belonged.

"Are you sure about this?" she asked, coming into the room behind him.

He swiped the bags she held from her hands and tossed them on the bed. Then he turned her toward the door and swatted her ass. "I'm hungry. Go fix me breakfast."

She frowned over her shoulder at him.

"Hurry, or I'm not taking you shopping later."

Her face brightened like the sun, and he ignored the flutter in his chest. Just what would he be willing to do for this woman? *Everything! I would kill for her.*

The sentiments embarrassed and annoyed him. He swung away from her and began unpacking her clothes. He hung the dresses in the closet and wondered what she would like to buy when they went shopping. Panties definitely. Could he get her into one of those shops that sold raunchier items? He hoped so. The dirty talking they'd done was blistering, and he intended to take it further. Shira was a fireball and hot as hell. He got a hard-on just thinking about her naked.

Shira

While he thought of bedroom antics they could get up to, his cell phone rang. He dug it out of his pocket and saw that it was his brother calling. He stabbed the connect button. "Alec, this better be important. There's a beautiful woman in my kitchen who I've decided to take on the counter next to the eggs and bacon."

"Wow, all kinds of detail I don't care to know," Alec said. "You sound disgustingly happy."

"Shut up."

"I'm sorry I have to call with the news I have."

Max stiffened. "What news?"

"Not only is Corbin not doing business with us, he's saying there's a rumor going around that we strong-armed Wilson into his deal, and Wilson is backing that up. I got a call from the DPOR who are investigating it."

"Are you shitting me?" Max ran a hand through his hair and began pacing.

"No, I think someone's behind it. I'm about to go over there and talk to Wilson myself."

Max thought he heard an exclamation from Shira like something upset her. "No, you can't go to him now that the DPOR is in it. We can talk to Mancini together to find out where he heard the rumor. If someone's gunning for us, they will be taken down. I'll pick you up in half an hour."

He ended the call and went to check on Shira. She stood by the refrigerator with her back to him, but it was clear that she was shaking. Max hurried to her and drew her against him. "Baby, what's wrong?"

She jumped and tried pulling away, but he held on. "N-Nothing." She smiled, but it was forced.

"What's going on, Shira? Tell me now."

She spun out of his hold, but he caught her wrist. When he tugged her to him, she lost the grip on her cell phone, and it began to fall. He moved with the easy speed that came to his kind and caught it. The horror and fear in her gaze as she looked at the phone told him volumes.

Max held Shira at his side while he flipped the phone open.

"Max, stop. Give it to me. I said nothing's going on," she insisted. "I just burned my finger. That's all."

He didn't smell any food cooking. She was lying to him. Anger welled in him, but not at the woman he'd chosen as his new mate, at whatever had caused her to be afraid to tell him the truth. The person who took away the happiness that had shown on Shira's sweet face would pay dearly.

He pressed the call button, and the number that came up wasn't one he recognized. Shira made a sound of alarm, but he ignored it. He pressed the call button again to connect. A familiar voice came on the line. "Have you decided to come to me, Shira? You made the right choice. Now I won't have to ruin your lover. Not entirely anyway."

Max had his answer of who was behind the sabotage of his and his brother's business. He gripped the phone in his hand so tightly he heard it crack. "I'm coming for you, Ellerby. Wait for me."

He tossed the phone on the floor and turned to Shira. She wrung her hands together, and tears collected in the corners of her eyes. "I have to go," she said.

He gripped her arms tighter. "No! Didn't you tell me you wouldn't leave me?"

She sniffed and shook her head. "I'm not leaving you." Anger sparked in her gaze. "He's not going to break us up. No, I have to leave and go to his house so I can get him straight. We're together now, and no amount of threats is going to change that."

Max smiled. He was proud of her, and she was cute with her determination and grit. Still, Max wasn't crazy enough to let her go anywhere near Ellerby. "I'm glad you feel that way, baby, but you're not going anywhere. I'm going to handle this, and you're going to wait here until I get back."

"Max—"

"Promise, Shira."

"No, I'm going! You can't stop me. I have to show Sam he can't intimidate me anymore." She continued outlining reasons she had to talk to Sam, to convince him to leave them alone. Max knew it would take more than words. For a moment he considered allowing Shira to go with him, but he changed his mind. He still needed to tell her about the shifting, and seeing it firsthand without warning wasn't the way to go about it. She needed to stay home.

"I have something very important to discuss with you when I get back," he said in a quiet tone. Shira fell silent. He watched her eyes widen and excitement spark there. He knew she jumped to conclusions, and he was okay with that. Shira was his mate, so whatever she wanted, he would give her. "Wait for me, please?"

She blew out a resigned breath and nodded. "Fine, but be careful." She reached up and stroked his cheek. Desire hit him between the eyes. What he wanted more than anything was to stay here and make love to her. From the way she trembled when he touched her, she felt the same. "I don't want him to hurt you."

"I promise he won't, and I'll come back soon."

Max kissed her and left the house on a jog. He hopped behind the wheel of his car and peeled out of the drive. First, he would pick up his brother, and then they would have a word or two with that scum Ellerby.

* * * *

"He's under the illusion that he's important," Alec commented when they pulled up to the house.

Max frowned. "You're sure this is the place? The way he comes off you'd think he would live in a mansion like Mancini's. This seems too…"

"Average?" Alec supplied. "My information isn't wrong. He's here. That's the car he was driving the other night at the party, and I'm picking up his scent."

Max agreed. He would never forget Ellerby's scent as long as he lived, and he'd better not pick it up after today within a five mile radius of Shira. "Let's go then. The sooner we put the fear of the leopard in him the better. I need to get back to Shira."

His brother eyed him but said nothing and slid from the car. Max met him on the other side, and they ascended the walk to the front door. Max leaned on the bell long and hard. He picked up the grumbling complaints on the other side of the door and schooled his face.

Sam Ellerby opened the door. "What the hell are you two doing here? If you think you're going to intimidate me, you're wrong. If you're foolish enough to—"

"Look at me, Ellerby," Max demanded. He let his eyes shift to that of the leopard. "Do I look impressed with you?"

Ellerby paled, blinked, and then scrubbed his eyes. He swung his gaze from Max to Alec, and his brother took a step forward to rest a clawed hand on Ellerby's shoulder. "Let's have a chat inside, shall we?"

Ellerby stuttered and stumbled backward. Max and Alec followed him inside and shut the door behind them.

"What-what-what," Ellerby stammered. "What kind of trick is this? How did you get your eyes to look like an animal's?"

"To be more specific, a leopard," Max corrected him.

His brother dug his claws in where he still held onto Ellerby's shoulder. Ellerby winced. "That's good makeup. Let go," he demanded of Alec.

Max's brother frowned. "Are you telling me what to do, Ellerby? I'm sure you're not afraid, right? An influential man like you? I mean you could make one phone call and ruin our reputation, cause us to lose close to a million dollars."

Alec backed him into his living room and shoved him down on the couch. Ellerby stayed where he was, staring in horror up at them. The most Max had done was shift his eyes, but it was enough for now. If Shira's ex didn't start changing his tune, Max was prepared to do much more, and Ellerby might not recover from it.

Max towered over the man with arms folded across his chest. "Now let's get this straight so there are no misunderstandings. You convinced Mancini not to do business with us. Our association with him is somewhat new, but you've known him a while. Am I right?"

Ellerby cleared his throat and tugged at his collar. "I met him a few years ago at a gathering Senator Jones was having in honor of his daughter."

"Oh a senator," Alec commented, although he didn't sound impressed. Neither was Max. Tossing around names was the kind of thing a small man like Ellerby did.

"Changing Mancini's mind wasn't enough. You went one step further and brought Wilson into it," Max continued. "I'm willing to bet that isn't the end of your plans though."

Belligerence set in Ellerby's expression, and he looked away saying nothing. Max leaned down and thumped the man's chest with the back of his hand. He pulled most of the strength at his command. A real blow would crack a human's bones with one hit. He let just enough through to drive the air out of Ellerby's lungs. Ellerby sputtered and coughed, trying to drag in a breath.

"Answer," Alec snapped.

"Y-Yes, but I won't..." All of a sudden Ellerby couldn't seem to think straight. Max supplied the words.

"You won't open your mouth to speak a word against me and my brother." He leaned down and brought his eyes level with Ellerby's. He allowed more of the leopard to come through, just enough for the color of his skin to shimmer and hint at the animal inside him. His nails grew to claws, and his teeth sharpened. Max allowed his jaw to grow slack so

Ellerby could see. A bite or a scratch could tear him to shreds. A sharp, foul scent burned Max's nose, and he glanced down. Ellerby had wet himself. Somehow he didn't feel sorry for the man. "You will correct the rumor you spread and set Wilson on the right path. If you come within a state of Shira, I'm sure you can guess what I will do—what my brother and I both will do."

"A *state*," Ellerby shrieked like a little girl. "I just moved back here. I just took this job."

"Sucks to be you, doesn't it, pal?" Alec growled.

Ellerby shrunk away from the animosity in Alec. "Okay, just please, don't... Don't kill me."

Max clamped his lips together to keep from laughing. They'd never killed anyone, and despite what Ellerby had said, they'd never pressured anyone into a business deal either.

"As you can see," Alec told him, "we're not your average businessmen. Don't cross us. Got it?"

"I got it," Ellerby muttered.

Max and Alec watched him for a little while longer, and then they turned to leave. When they were back in the car and driving down the highway, Max let out the laughter he'd held in check, and his brother joined him.

When they sobered, Alec glanced over at him, growing serious. "Have you told her about your ability?"

Max knew he was talking about Shira and them not being human. "I'm heading back to tell her now." He gripped the steering wheel until his knuckles turned white. "I never believed I could have another mate, but I'm beginning to think she's it. I can see myself with her forever. But if she—"

"Don't. She will accept you. From what I've seen, she loves you, and you—"

"I want to protect her. I don't want her ever to be hurt again."

Alec grinned. "Fine. Anyway, I'm sure everything will work out great. She's not going to let the fact that you grow a little extra hair once in a while and get a penchant for running in the wild get between you."

"I hope you're right."

Max dropped his brother off, waved to Whisper who stood in the doorway of his house, and drove toward home. With each mile he covered, the tension in his neck increased. He ran a hand over it and massaged the muscles. Dread settled in the pit of his stomach, but he wouldn't put this off. He should have told Shira before she said she would stay. She had a right to know everything about him—especially the way he felt about her.

When he walked in the door, intense joy displaced his nervousness seeing her waiting for him. He held out his arms, and she darted across the floor to settle into his embrace. He tipped her chin up to kiss her soft lips. She tasted like honey, and his heart swelled. *I can't believe her power over me.*

"Shira, I need to tell you something."

A tremor passed over her, and he caressed her shoulders, trying to soothe her. He hesitated and then took the plunge. "Baby, I love you."

Her sharp intake of breath was the only sound in the room. "What? You… I never thought…" Tears spilled down her cheeks, and she wiped them away almost violently. "You love me? You really do? You're not just saying that?"

He shook his head. "No, I wouldn't say it if it wasn't true. It took me by surprise, and I thought it wasn't possible for my kind to mate more than once."

She wrinkled her nose. "Have sex more than once?"

He chuckled. "No, have *a* mate." He put her from him and then led her to a chair to sit down. "That's the other part of what I need to tell you. First, am I right in believing you love me too?"

"Do you even have to ask?" Her smile lit up his world, and he was hard-pressed not to forget the conversation and take her into his arms.

Her light-hearted laugh made him join in. "Yes, Max Macgregor, I love you so much!"

Max dropped to one knee and took her hands. The wideness in her eyes told him he'd made her jump to the wrong conclusion. He refused to take it back seeing the fluttery movements in her hands and the spark in her gaze.

"Do you remember the leopard you saw?" he began.

Her brows dropped low in confusion, but she nodded.

Max gripped her fingers and brought them to his lips. He kissed each one, feeling her shiver with every touch. How the hell did he tell her and hope she wouldn't panic, thinking he was a psycho like her ex? Showing her might frighten her, and that was the last thing he wanted. Shira had had enough fear in her life.

He sparked on an idea.

"Do you remember when you were running in the trees that night at the party and about how confused you were about which way to go?"

"How did you know about that?"

He didn't answer her question right away but continued with his line of questioning. "What did you feel when you saw the leopard?"

"I was kind of relieved," she said. "I know you'll think I'm crazy, but I feel like he's my protector, my friend. If I had any sense I'd call animal control and have them pick him up. He shouldn't be running free around residential areas. I wonder if a circus lost him."

Max jiggled her hands to call her attention back to him. "Focus, baby."

She chuckled. "Sorry. Anyway, I suppose I trusted him. He led me back to the street and to your brother. Alec said he knew the leopard."

Max nodded. He rubbed her fingers. "Shira, that leopard was me."

She blinked at him. "Oh, you mean, the way I feel about him, and that you'll protect me? I know. I trust you, and I know you won't let anyone hurt me."

"No." He released her hands and stood up, then backed away.

When he began removing his clothes, she focused on his body. His cock went erect as he saw the interest in her gaze. This wasn't the time to get excited, but he couldn't help it. The woman he loved looked like she wanted to have him for lunch, and he didn't mind at all.

When he was naked in front of her, she reached out to his cock, but he caught her hands. "Whoa, baby, I'll never do this if you start that."

"Do what?"

He shifted. No pretense, no warning. Shira surged to her feet and slapped a hand over her mouth. "Oh my goodness!"

He didn't move a muscle in case he scared her. In fact, he did all he could not to appear threatening. To his surprise, she dropped to her knees and threw her arms around his neck, sobbing. "I can't believe it. I just can't believe it. I must be dreaming. Max, you're the leopard? I knew it wasn't natural to be so drawn to a wild animal like that! Wow! This is amazing."

He shifted back to his human form and sat on the carpet, pulling Shira onto his lap. "Wait, you're not afraid?"

"Of course not." She grinned. "It's you isn't it?"

"It's me," he affirmed.

"Incredible." She kept touching his skin, ran fingers through his hair, and stared at him in awe. "You're amazing."

Warmth spread over Max's insides. "No, *you* are. Marry me, Shira."

She gaped. "But we've just met."

"Marry me," he said again. "This time I won't let my mate get away without claiming her in every sense of the word. Be my wife."

She hesitated and ducked her head. "Are you sure you want me? I can't be like *her*."

"I've never been more sure." He raised her chin. "I love you for you, and I know you are the one for me. Shira, you've taken my heart, and I won't ask for it back."

"Then, yes, I will marry you, Max, because you've taken my heart, too, and you'll always have it."

TWIN LEOPARDS – Tressie Lockwood

She threw her arms around his shoulders and pressed her breasts to his bare chest. Max felt her nipples tighten, and he moaned. "Now I can take you freely."

"Yes, you can." She grinned at him and then stood up. Her pussy was in line with his face, and Max's mouth watered as she began removing her clothes. Happiness surged within him along with desire. He never imagined his life would take this much of a turn for the better. He'd been down on everything and everyone, and a few weeks ago, he wouldn't have believed a woman as perfect for him as Shira would come into his life. She was here now, and he had no intention of letting her go.

When she was naked, he reached out and ran a finger down the slit of her pussy. She was already wet, and he tasted her juices. He wanted to eat her out, but that would take control, something which was missing at the moment. Instead, he tugged her back to his lap. As she descended, he guided his already stiff cock between her legs. She sank slowly onto it, and a hiss of breath left his lips. Up to the hilt, he fit in her warm channel. Her inner muscles clenched around his member, milked it. He arched his hips and drove into her while cupping her ass. Shira pumped hard, her eyes closed and head thrown back. She murmured his name, and each time she did, his cock pulsed and seemed to grow harder. Shira's slender form sent him insane. He couldn't stop kissing her skin, licking it, and enjoying the feel of her squirming on his cock. Everything about his lover brought him to the edge of an orgasm, and he willed himself to fall.

"Shira, baby, you're going to make me explode."

"Do it, Max. I want it so bad," she purred. "I want to feel your come in me."

That was all she needed to say. He ran his hands up her back, pressed his fingers to her soft skin, and crushed her to him. He devoured her delicious mouth and thrust his tongue in to taste her. With his fingers tangled in her hair, he took what was all his and no other man's. He ground deep into her pussy, and made her bounce on his erection until the sensations were more than he could stand. She screamed, and the spasms in her thigh muscles told him she had come. Just a few more thrusts and Max let go. He came strong and hard, shaken from head to toe as he emptied himself inside of her.

When he was done and they had calmed somewhat, Max held onto Shira and stood with her in his arms. He carried her into his bedroom and kicked the door shut. What he would do now was to spend the rest of the day giving Shira and himself pleasure to make up for all the pain that came before. From then on, nothing would come between them, and he would be all the protection she needed.

The End

About the Author

Tressie Lockwood has always loved books, and she enjoys writing about heroines who are overcoming the trials of life. She writes straight from her heart, reaching out to those who find it hard to be completely themselves no matter what anyone else thinks. She hopes her readers enjoy her short stories. Visit Tressie on the web at: www.tressielockwood.blogspot.com.

Printed in Great Britain
by Amazon.co.uk, Ltd.,
Marston Gate.